the Dublin Revi

number fifty-three | WINTER 2013–14

GW00359408

EDITOR & PUBLISHER: BRENDAN BARRINGTON
DEPUTY PUBLISHER: DEANNA ORTIZ

The Dublin Review, number fifty-three (Winter 2013–14).
Design by Atelier David Smith. Printed by Naas Printing Ltd.

ISBN 978-0-9569925-7-4

The Dublin Review is published quarterly. Editorial and business correspondence to The Dublin Review, P.O. Box 7948, Dublin 1, Ireland, or to enquiry@thedublinreview.com. The Dublin Review welcomes submissions, which should take the form of printed typescript only and should be submitted by post. Please supply your postal and email addresses. If you wish to have the manuscript returned in the event that your work is not accepted, please enclose an appropriately sized self-addressed stamped envelope or, if you live outside the Republic of Ireland, a self-addressed envelope with an adequate number of International Reply coupons. (Irish postal rates may be checked at www.anpost.ie.) The Dublin Review assumes no responsibility for unsolicited material.

Visit our website: www.thedublinreview.com

SUBSCRIPTIONS: €34 / UK£26 per year (Ireland & NI), €45 / UK£36 / US$60 per year (rest of world). Institutions add €15 / UK£13 / US$20. To subscribe or to order back issues, please use the secure-ordering facility at www.thedublinreview.com. Alternatively, you may send your address and a cheque or Visa/MC data to Subscriptions, The Dublin Review, P.O. Box 7948, Dublin 1, Ireland. Credit-card orders are billed at the euro price. Please indicate if credit-card billing address differs from mailing address.

TRADE SALES: The Dublin Review is distributed to the trade by Gill & Macmillan Distribution, Hume Avenue, Park West, Dublin 12.

SALES REPRESENTATION: Robert Towers, 2 The Crescent, Monkstown, Co. Dublin, tel +353 1 2806532, fax +353 1 2806020.

The Dublin Review receives financial assistance from the Arts Council.

Contents | *number fifty-three* | WINTER 2013–14

Turf wars

RACHEL ANDREWS

1

On the morning of 19 June 2012, in the company of a number of other men, Michael Darcy drove turf-cutting equipment onto Clonmoylan Bog, near the shore of Lough Derg in south-east Co. Galway. Darcy, a heavy-set man in his forties, works as contractor cutting turf for households on Clonmoylan and other bogs.

Darcy and the other men were being observed by rangers of the National Parks and Wildlife Service (NPWS). At around 11.30 that morning, the rangers called gardaí to the scene. The turf cutters were asked to stop what they were doing and leave the bog. A stand-off ensued, and went on throughout the day, with gardaí maintaining a presence on the bog and the turf cutters refusing to leave. Determined to force the issue, Darcy used a group text messaging service to contact turf cutters in other areas of the country. People arrived at Clonmoylan from Roscommon, Laois, Kildare, and from as far away as Kerry and Cavan. By around 8 p.m., when gardaí announced they were seizing the turf-cutting machinery, there were about a hundred protesters on the bog. The protest continued to swell as the night went on.

Like most Irish lowland bogs, Clonmoylan – or Cloonmoylan, as it is alternatively spelled – is a 'raised' bog. As the glaciers retreated from the Irish midlands after the Ice Age, they left behind a bumpy landscape with poor drainage. The depressions filled with water, creating thousands of tiny lakes. Over the ten thousand years that followed, peat was deposited and built up on the lake beds, eventually emerging above the surface, where it was covered with thick cushions of bog-mosses. Peat is composed mainly of partially decayed wetland vegetation, and it accumulates slowly, at a rate of around one millimetre per year. Raised bogs, if left to their own devices, are about 95 per cent water. Turf cutters build and maintain drains in bogs in order to reduce the water content and facilitate extraction of peat for fuel; but this also has dramatic effects on the ecology of the bog, and eventually causes it to stop growing.

In 1992 Ireland, along with the other EU member states, signed the Habitats Directive, which set out criteria for states to designate areas of scientific or environmental importance as Special Areas of Conservation, or SACs. Ireland's raised boglands, valued for their distinctive ecology, were under pressure from forestry, agricultural reclamation, drainage, and mechanized cutting. A scientific survey led to thirty-two raised bogland sites being proposed for designation as SACs in 1997. That same year, the Habitats Directive was signed into Irish law. By June, the government had changed and the new Minister for the Arts, Heritage, Gaeltacht and the Islands, Síle de Valera, announced an immediate ban on turf cutting on the raised-bog SACs. But the ban was not enforced, and cutting took place in the 1998 season.

In February 1999, following a series of consultations with turf cutters who raised concerns about property rights being forfeited, about access to fuel supplies, and about the loss of a way of life during the spring and summer months when cutting traditionally takes place, the Minister announced a ten-year derogation whereby owners of bogland and holders of turbary rights – i.e. the right to cut turf on land owned by someone else – would be allowed to continue exploiting the designated bogs. The use of 'sausage machines', which cause particular damage to bogs by creating deep, long crevices that drain them of water, was banned on SACs, but other forms of mechanical extraction continued to be permitted. In a statement on the derogation, Minister de Valera said she had decided to make 'exceptional arrangements in the case of cutters for domestic use'. These cutters, she said, would be given 'a period of up to ten years to make new arrangements'. In a separate paragraph, the Minister said those who have been cutting 'for their own personal domestic use' would be permitted to cut 'the amount of turf needed for their own use only for up to ten years in less sensitive areas of the bog'.

Given the choice between the Minister's references to 'domestic use' and 'their own personal domestic use', turf cutters unsurprisingly preferred the broader definition implied by the former, and the state made no serious attempt to ensure that turf was being cut solely for 'personal' use. A 2006 report carried out by the scientific research branch of the NPWS found that it had 'become difficult to distinguish between legitimate domestic cutting and small-scale commercial operations'. The same report also found that, contrary to the terms of the derogation, turf cutting had been effectively allowed to continue even in the most sensitive areas of the designated bogs; and that the stipulation that turf cutters must seek ministerial permission before cutting on SACs had never been enforced.

For ten years or more, the vast majority of turf cutters continued to operate as they had always done, and the government buried its head in the sand. In January 2011, the European Commission – which had monitored the situation in Ireland with growing frustration – threatened court action over the state's failure to protect SAC bogs. The threat – which could have led to Ireland facing daily fines of up to €25,000 – finally forced the government to take the issue seriously. The government established the Irish Peatlands Council to oversee the protection and conservation of the boglands, and on 2 June 2011 it convened an emergency meeting with turf cutters in Ballinasloe, Co. Galway. A deal was struck whereby no more turf would be cut that summer on the designated bogs, while both sides agreed to work together to identify non-SAC sites to which turf cutters could relocate their work. Those who stopped cutting on the SACs and did not relocate would be able to avail of a compensation package of €1,000 per year, plus free annual delivery of ten tonnes of turf, for a maximum of fifteen years. (The compensation has since been raised to €1,500 and fifteen tonnes of turf per year for fifteen years, with adjustments for inflation.) At the time, the agreement to stop cutting pertained to the thirty-two raised bogs originally designated as SACs in 1997; a cutting ban on a further twenty-three bogs, designated as SACs in 2002 after the EU found Ireland had originally designated too little of its raised-bog habitat for protection, was due to be enforced from the end of 2011.

2

According to the *Atlas of the Irish Rural Landscape**, bogs cover one-sixth of Ireland's total land area. But within the category 'peatand' there is great ecological variety, and one of the most important determinants of the ecology of a bog is the degree to which it has been exploited for fuel.

Ireland has more than half of the raised bogland remaining in the EU, but it is an ecosystem under increasing threat. Figures vary regarding the extent of 'active' – i.e. peat-forming – raised bog that remains in Ireland today, but most research indicates it is only around 50,000 hectares, less than 1 per cent of the amount we once had. Over the past thirty years around 260,000 hectares of raised bog has been damaged as a result of mechanized cutting. (The other main form of peatland in Ireland, blanket bog, occurs mainly on high ground; apart from turf cutting, the main threat to blanket bogs comes from overgrazing, and a number of blanket bogs too have been granted SAC status.) Bogland is subject to the Habitats Directive because it supports a unique range of plant and animal life. Bogs are also carbon sinks, holding roughly half of the carbon stored in Irish soils, and another reason environmentalists wish to protect them is that the draining and cutting of bogland, and the burning of turf (on a large scale in power stations, as well as domestically), releases significant quantities of greenhouse gases into the atmosphere. According to an article written in 2009 for the *Irish Times* by Dr David Wilson, researcher at the school of biology and environmental science

*Second edition (Cork University Press, 2011), edited by F.H.A. Aalen, Kevin Whelan and Matthew Stout.

in University College Dublin and an adviser to the EPA on peatlands management, the cutting and burning of bogland releases about 2.5 million tonnes of carbon a year – roughly equal to the annual quantity of carbon emitted by cars on Irish roads.

The bog, suggests the *Atlas of the Rural Irish Landscape*, has been 'etched as deeply into the human as into the physical record in Ireland, to an extent unrivalled in Europe'. 'Saving' turf from the edges of bogs by hand-cutting has been a feature of Irish rural life for many centuries. By the late eighteenth century, peat was the primary source of fuel in Ireland. But by the end of the nineteenth century, English coal, which was of better quality and consistency, was widely available on the Irish market, and the use of turf became increasingly confined to impoverished peatland areas.

Farmers and other land users cut turf by hand using the *slean*, a tool consisting of an iron blade mounted on a wooden shaft. Turf cutters spread the freshly cut sods about the turf bank to allow then to dry and stiffen. After a week or two they returned to the bog to 'foot' the semi-dry turf, standing the sods upright in small stacks of five or six, allowing air to circulate through them. After another week or two they returned to the bogs and made large piles of turf out of the 'footings'; this completed the drying process, and by this time the sods would often have shrunk to one third their original size and weight.

Turf cutting is not farming; it is extraction of a finite resource, more akin to coal mining or oil drilling. But because of the long history of small-scale turf-cutting in a rural setting in Ireland, the activity is generally viewed as part of a benign agricultural tradition. In a 2012 paper on the public value of peatlands, UCD researchers found that bogs are seen as important for, among other things, their 'coexistence with farmed areas in which whole communities would once have cut turf together during the summer months'.* This is despite the fact that private turf cutting in Ireland has increasingly become outsourced and mechanized: owners of bogland or tur-

*Craig Bullock, Marcus Collier and Frank J. Convery, 'Peatlands, their public good value and priorities for their future management – the example of Ireland', Land Use Policy no. 29, 2012.

bary rights hire contractors, like Michael Darcy, to cut their peat by machine.

The mechanization of domestic turf cutting is a relatively recent development, long preceded by the industrial exploitation of bogland by the Irish state. The Turf Development Board, established in 1934, was empowered to make compulsory purchase of boglands. The onset of the Second World War caused coal imports to fall dramatically, and the TDB promoted private turf production, drained 24,000 acres of its own bogland, and commenced producing machine-cut turf.

In 1946, the TDB was renamed Bord na Móna. Its First Development Programme provided for two ESB peat-fired power stations and the development of twenty-four bogs to produce over a million tonnes of turf per year. In 1950, the Second Development Programme provided for four more power stations and set substantial targets for the production of milled peat – turf in crumb or powder form. Bord na Móna came to own nearly half the raised bogland in the midlands, and the electrification of rural Ireland was powered in large part by peat extracted in rural Ireland. The number of peat-fired ESB plants topped out at seven between 1965 and 1988. In the absence of coal or petroleum deposits, turf became Ireland's indigenous industrial fossil fuel.

Bord na Móna remains the dominant peat producer in the country, extracting around four million tonnes annually, according to the Irish Peatlands Conservation Council (IPCC). Almost all of this is milled peat, supplied to the ESB for power generation or used by Bord na Móna in the manufacturing of peat briquettes. In the larger bogs exploited by Bord na Móna, drains are set fifteen metres apart, creating long parallel production fields, each around one kilometre in length. The surface is broken and milled into peat crumbs that are then turned over, or harrowed, by a series of spoons towed behind a tractor, and left to dry in the sun and wind. When the peat crumbs are half-dried, they are gathered into ridges in the centre of each field, and lifted and dropped on top of ridges on the adjoining field, until five ridges have been accumulated into a single large ridge that is lifted into a storage stockpile. The stockpile field receives the peat crops from ten fields, five on either side.

When the production season is over, the stockpiles are covered to keep them dry, until they are loaded into wagons and transported by specially built narrow-gauge railway to factories or power stations. The seven original peat-fired power plants have all been decommissioned, and electricity is now generated from peat at three newer plants: the ESB stations at Shannonbridge in west Co. Offaly and Lough Ree in Co. Longford, and Edenderry Power Plant in Co. Offaly, which burns turf and biomass. The role of turf in supplying Ireland's electricity needs has been in steady decline, but remains substantial; currently, according to the International Energy Agency, around 8 per cent of Ireland's electricity generation is fuelled by peat.

The Bord na Móna boglands are strange, eerie places. The decades of peat extraction have left a kind of black devastation in the landscape. Driving across the midlands by certain routes, it is possible to be surrounded by the seemingly endless Bord na Móna bogs, vast expanses of nothingness, land meeting sky. The history of the industrial exploitation of the Irish peatlands is already well past its midpoint; Bord na Móna estimates it has twenty years' cutting left on the midland bogs.

As part of the Habitats Directive, agreements were made in 1999 that industrial extraction should end on designated sites. Bord na Móna's interest in SACs – around twenty sites, according to the IPCC – was bought out by the NPWS at a cost of around €23 million, with the EU paying three quarters of the cost for seven thousand hectares of Bord na Móna land, including four thousand hectares of SAC-designated uncut peatland. Companies that were extracting moss peat from other SAC bogs were also bought out by the NPWS. The EU also supplied funding to the semi-state forestry company Coillte to help it remove trees and block up drains on the SAC peatland sites it owned.

Bord na Móna is currently moving away from peat extraction into waste management, the generation of wind power, and other areas: it terms this its 'new contract with nature'.

3

While the Irish state has largely succeeded in ushering Bord na Móna and the handful of other big industrial players off the SAC bogs, it has had no such success with the smaller turf cutters.

According to Michael Darcy, he had had two encounters with the NPWS over his work on Clonmoylan bog prior to the stand-off in June 2012. When we spoke a couple of weeks after the stand-off, he told me that about ten years earlier the NPWS had threatened him with a High Court injunction if he did not stop cleaning drains on Clonmoylan. According to Darcy, the bog had been drained originally between 1985 and 1986, after he received an EU grant for the purpose; now, EU environmental policy dictated that the EU-subsidized drains must no longer be maintained. With the derogation for domestic turf cutters in place, and restrictions only loosely enforced, it seems probable that the NPWS suspected Darcy was preparing the bogs for more than domestic cutting. Darcy told me that he put the NPWS under notice that he would wait three weeks and then return to the bogs. No High Court injunction materialized; he decided the NPWS had been 'kind of bluffing', and went back to working on the drains and cutting turf as usual the following summer.

After that, Darcy said, he heard nothing more on the subject until 24 May 2011. He was cutting turf in Clonmoylan, by the side of the main road, when two rangers from the NPWS, accompanied by a local armed Garda detective and a sergeant, told him he was involved in illegal cutting and that he should get off the bog as fast as he could. Darcy was adamant that he had never been officially notified of the designation of Clonmoylan as an SAC. This may seem hard to credit, given that the designation was made in 1997, but turf cutters across the country have frequently made such claims. A report by the chairman of the Peatlands Forum, Mr Justice John Quirke, cited disputes over when and how landowners and those working on the bogs were notified about the SAC designations and the turf-cutting ban as a major factor in the breakdown in trust between local communities and the state agencies.

In May 2011, on being told he was breaking the law, Darcy downed his tools and left Clonmoylan bog.

4

In early July 2012, a couple of weeks after Michael Darcy and like-minded turf cutters from around the country made their stand against the gardaí and the NPWS, I drove to Clonmoylan to meet with him. He took me to a crossroads not far from the bog, where there was a smallish road leading off the main R352 and where a small church stood a short distance away. 'Here is where your boots were searched and your pockets and everything going to the protest,' he said. On the day I met him, Darcy was accompanied by Francis Donohue, a teacher who has become involved with the turf cutters' cause. Donohue told me that at one point forty Garda cars were parked at the cross-roads, blocking people from making their way to the protest, forcing them to cross dark, wet fields in the middle of the night, using their phones to illuminate the way. The protest continued throughout the night and into the early morning, until a deal was brokered around 8 a.m. between turf-cutter representatives, two local councillors, the gardaí and the NPWS. Teresa Mannion and a camera crew from RTE stayed with the turf cutters all night, documenting the torrential rain that fell on unprepared protesters: many of them had come out in shirt sleeves, for it had been a warm, fine evening and it wasn't until dark that the clouds rolled in and the rain began to tumble down.

Darcy and Donohue walked me down the road from the crossroads, and over a narrow bridge to the place where the turf cutters gathered. They pointed to a charred patch where some of them had built a small fire by the roadside; they showed me a large tree others stood under when the rain started. At one point, a large slab of polystyrene, around eight feet square, was passed around, and as many of the protesters as possible got in under it. The turf cutters termed the event a 'siege', and trenchantly maintained it was they who were being put under pressure. The gardaí, and most particularly the NPWS rangers, who were prevented by the crowd from removing Michael Darcy's machinery from the site, and two of whose members remained in their jeep throughout the night, surrounded by the protesters, were emphatically the villains of the piece.

I asked Darcy and Donohue about published claims by Tony Lowes, director of Friends of the Irish Environment (FIE), that the NPWS officials had been 'trapped in their jeep' by protesters, had 'lights shone at them' and 'sods of turf thrown at the car'. They batted the claims away, and claimed that Lowes was the 'right-hand man' of the NPWS.

5

Tony Lowes has been an environmental activist since the early 1990s. American by birth, he studied at Trinity College Dublin in the 1970s and has lived in Ireland, more or less, ever since, even allowing himself at one point to become stateless in order to stay in the country. In May 2012 Lowes raised money for Friends of the Irish Environment to hire a private plane and take aerial photographs of illegal cutting on protected bogs. The images, of bogs in counties Galway, Kildare, Roscommon and Westmeath, are all of a piece – strips of brown and black turf plots spreading out from a central area of raised bog, a debased landscape, unhappy even to the disinterested eye.

Lowes and his organization have also appeared twice, in November 2011 and September 2012, before the Petitions Committee in Brussels to urge it to put pressure on the Irish government over the issue; the Committee, which hears cases brought by EU citizens on matters that affect them, is due to carry out an investigation into the petition. Small wonder I saw signs mounted in Clonmoylan, red lettering on white background, that warned: 'Tony Lowes and F.I.E friends, Keep Out'.

I went to meet Lowes one sparkling August afternoon at his home in Eyeries, in West Cork, a beautiful, almost magical location by the sea. Speaking in a voice so low I later strained to hear it on the recorder, he came across as something very different from the aggressive force the turf cutters had depicted. Indeed, he was sympathetic towards the smaller turf contractors and landowners, suggesting that it is the bigger industrial peat-extracting companies – some of whom, he asserts, are operating with neither planning permission nor licence – who are doing the most damage. 'It's hard not to understand them,' he said of the domestic turf cutters, 'but the problem is that they are [cutting on] designated bogs and the law says they can't cut on them.'

The law, of course, is what is in dispute. Across protected boglands, where turf cutting is now illegal, signs and posters have been erected. 'Private property, No Entry to National Parks and Wildlife Service,' they say. Or: 'The bogs, the valleys, the streams, belong to the Irish people.' Or: 'Forbidden Ground.' There is something primal and simplistic about such sentiments, but the turf cutters also make more measured and specific arguments against the way the state has handled the matter. In Clonmoylan, Darcy and Donohue showed me a part of the bog, divided by a road, one half of which was excluded from SAC status due to the 'naturally occurring' boundary of the road. Turf cutters contend the road is manmade, and that the bog in question was excluded because it lapped the river's edge; the ESB, they allege, wanted it for what are known as 'fishing rights' – rights that allow it to preserve and develop the fishery on a specific river area.

Lowes agreed the designation process had been flawed – he has seen instances of large commercial contractors operating beside SACs where there is also a road on one side or another, which is 'just nonsense' – and FIE has identified at least 160 additional sites that it says ought to have been protected. Many of these sites, FIE states, are exploited today by private industrial contractors extracting peat for the horticulture trade.

In a case study undertaken in 2009 and 2010, the FIE investigated the unregulated extraction by an industrial company of peat from raised bogs in Co. Westmeath, reporting that 'during one hour we saw three large articulated lorry loads of peat soil leave the site' and a pump pumping vast quantities of sediment-laden water into the neighbouring River Inny and into the Special Protection Area of Lough Derrravargh downstream. In 2009 it presented this report to the Shannon Regional Fisheries Board, the NPWS, Westmeath County Council and the EPA, but according to the FIE's website no action has yet been taken, and the unregulated extraction of peat continues across Ireland.

6

The Turf Cutters and Contractors Association (TCCA) has opposed the state's approach to the protection of bogs in almost every particular – going all the way back to the EU's Habitats Directive itself, which it has described as 'unlawful'. At the 2011 general election its spokesman Luke 'Ming' Flanagan was elected to represent Roscommon–South Leitrim. Some of its positions – for example, its 2009 assertion that the state's requirement that people 'surrender the equivalent of an oil well in their localities to faceless technocrats' was 'ethnic cleansing of the population from the most deprived areas of Ireland' – are eccentric; others are what you'd expect from any trade organization whose members face a serious threat to their livelihood, and which hopes to negotiate the most advantageous possible settlement. There is little doubt that the state has played its hand very badly. It was never going to be easy to compel people give up a long-standing source of fuel and income in exchange for modest financial compensation, or else to relocate to distant, unfamiliar and possibly inferior bogs; but in its failure to communicate clearly with bogland communities the agencies of the state have made the task even more difficult. 'Most [turf cutters] registered dismay and deep offence at what they perceived as a failure by the state and its agencies to communicate with them and provide them with adequate notice, advice, information or assistance in respect of what they perceive to be a measure which will deprive them of a vital, natural resource situated on or near their homes or properties and which forms a fundamental part of their livelihood, their sustenance and their heritage,' wrote Mr Justice Quirke in his report on the Peatlands Forum. Quirke also said that determination was now required, on the part of the state and its agencies, to 'accommodate communities whose lives and lifestyles have been gravely disrupted by measures and circumstances over which they have had no control and to provide them with monetary or other compensation for the sacrifices they have been prepared to make'.

The TCCA has successfully framed the cessation of turf-cutting as a case of individual turf-cutters being ordered, for no good reason, to cease doing work they have always done. For example, after the Clonmoylan protest the *Galway City Tribune* wrote that 'ordinary people – law-abiding citizens – find themselves subjected to the full rigours of the law for continuing to do something that their fathers and forefathers did before them'. The TCCA's campaign is undoubtedly being driven by those who have most to lose: the contractors. But the organization has also spoken for those in Irish bogland communities – often elderly and impoverished – who depend on turf from SAC bogs to heat their homes. 'Their only dignity and independence derives from the energy independence afforded by having their own turf banks,' the TCCA argued in a 2009 submission to the Working Group on the Cessation of Turf Cutting. The cost of converting their homes to oil or gas heating would, it claimed, exceed the state's modest annual compensation offer. (The NPWS says that to date, more than 2,800 applications have been received from turf-cutters and turbary rights holders wishing to join the compensation scheme, and more than €6 million has been paid out in compensation.) In their 2012 paper, the UCD researchers found that turf was being used to heat around 20,000 homes, mostly in rural areas and mostly those of less well-off families, who cannot afford to switch to gas or oil. The report also suggested that the introduction of a modest carbon tax in 2009 had made little difference to the use of turf in these households. Insofar as peat is either cut directly by house-holders or bought from contractors via the black economy, the tax actually incentivized its use.

The Quirke report, issued in March 2012, observed that a 'lengthy and probably tortuous process of discussion, negotiation and accommodation with every person and party affected by the relevant designations will be required over what may well be a protracted period of time'. A national plan, which was committed to by the government in the same month, is 'being worked on right now', according to the NPWS, and NPWS liaison officers have been appointed as points of contact regarding the relocation issue. However, in the summer of 2013 a significant amount of illegal turf cutting once again took place on bogs in Co. Galway, Co. Roscommon, and else-where, with the FIE claiming gardaí stood 'idly by', watching from the public road as the cutting began.

A member of the Kildare Turf Cutters Association emailed me a script pre-pared for the use of John Dore, spokesperson for cutters working on Mouds Bog in that county, during an interview on a local radio station. According to the script, in the absence of an acceptable solution to the 'so-called ban' on cutting in SAC bogs, turf cutters on Mouds Bog have since 2012 'continued to exercise their rights' to cut turf on forty banks. The script was also disparaging of the government's compensation package, claiming that no turf cutter on Mouds Bog had signed up for compensation and 'anybody doing so should be committed to a mental institution'.

7

In early January 2013, I returned to Clonmoylan Bog on my own. In the pale of winter, it felt more abandoned than it had in the wind and rain of the previous July, caught in a cool, ethereal beauty. Skeletal trees framed the road I had walked with the turf cutters, there was gorse and bracken along its edge, and the harsh, spiking grass had turned yellow and white in the fields, although out on the high dome of the bog I could see a mass of purple and brown and green. There was nobody about, but I saw six or seven yellow skip bags filled with cut turf, while a new notice had been posted near the entrance. It said: 'Cut Turf / Yes We Will / Yes We Can'.

The bog was sodden from heavy rainfall and squelched under my feet. The turf bank was six or seven feet high, and it was surrounded by a kind of moat filled with mucky peat and water. I wanted to get out onto the high bog and I thought about crossing the moat, skipping as best I could across it. I tried, tentatively, pressing my foot against the mudded ground and easily, too easily, I began to sink into it. Thinking better of it, I turned away. As I walked back – the cutaway part of the bog began around twenty metres or so from the roadside – I noticed a deep, excavated drain, again around six or seven feet high, shrouded by trees and weeds, but not blocked off, surely still in use.

I kept going along the narrow road, following the route I had walked with the turf cutters the previous summer, from the entrance of the bog down the winding roadway and past the different turf plots – one of them owned, they'd told me, by a blind, elderly priest who comes out every autumn to foot his own turf. Many of the plots to my left, which had been green and empty in the summer when no cutting was taking place, were now filled with small mounds of black turf sods.

I walked on, past the private field where Michael Darcy's machinery had been moved on the evening of the protest, in order that the NPWS should not be able to confiscate it – although rangers did, eventually, do so – and past the spot where Michael Darcy's digger went on fire later that night, sometime around 3 a.m.; the sight of this led to his collapse and hospitalization, and turf cutters' assertions, in hushed tones, that *somebody* must have set the digger on fire, and it certainly wasn't them.

I came out to the clearing where many of the protesters had stood, and where the NPWS jeep had been parked. I noticed another sign, one I hadn't seen before. 'SAC', it said, 'Interference unwarranted. Our Turbary Rights will not be untitled.'

I heard a noise, and looked up to the sky. Overhead was a flock of birds. As they turned, the evening sun glinted on their white underbellies. They rose and fell and pulled apart. Then they floated away into the clouds, wings tipped and burnished by the soft orange glow.

The note

CORMAC JAMES

I want to write to my uncle. I ought to have written to him long ago. More precisely, I ought to have written to him right at the start, just after it happened, when likely he wouldn't even have opened my letter, because of the grief. When, even if he had managed to open and read it, none of the words would have sunk in, because of the grief. The grief, just then, like a drug in his brain, bringing welcome stupidity, I tell myself. His eyes would have passed over the words blindly and the thing would have been done. That's when I should have written, when it didn't much matter what you wrote. At a time like that you could write (I could have written) the bluntest platitudes, that would not make (would not have made) the slightest impression.

I should have, but I didn't. (Familiar line.) I blame my younger self. He should have done his duty, taken courage and taken his chance, rather than hesitating interminably, then leaving the mess to me. I'd like to get hold of him and force him, right here and now, to do what he should have done a year ago. Better: I'd like to have it done by someone else entirely. Yes, that's more like it. I want someone else to write that – my – letter, to my uncle, whose son died / is dead. Even though he (the son) was / would be the same age as me, I didn't actually know him very well, so I don't have anything particular to say, which fact should perhaps make or have made the task easier, but did not. If truth be known, I've never even managed to make myself think too long about the wording, the actual words. All I wanted was for that letter to be written, and sent, and read (or not), and instantly forgotten, and my duty done. Not only did I never write it, I never even began, not knowing what to say, or how to say it – what length, tone, pitch, all that. I didn't know what you say in such circumstances. What do you say to a man the same age as your father, who like your father had an only son, your age, who's just died? Of course by your age I mean your age when he died. Worse: what do you say to a man who's just lost his only son in a meaningless way (his words) thanks to a freak infection (their words) after a minor (their word) surgical procedure? I didn't know what to say to such a man, in such circumstances. And it didn't seem fair, that I should be expected to know. After all, I was the child, and he a father. Who looks to a child for comfort? Shouldn't it always be the other way round? Isn't that the natural order of things?

Not knowing what to say to such a man, I've said nothing, and it's that silence more than his grief that I need to address now. I want to paper over my silence, you could say, if you wanted to play with words. That's what I need my letter to do. I want it written as it should be written, by someone who knows just what to say in such circumstances – someone who's been through this kind of thing time and again, and who knows from bitter experience just what to say, and says it well, just the right length, in just the right tone, and take the credit myself if the thing be nicely done, and feel absolved of all responsibility if somehow the letter fails to strike exactly the right note.

The grave of the Jews

PHILIP Ó CEALLAIGH

1

It is late November 2012, and I am in the home of Vasile Enache in the small village of Cuza Vodă, in eastern Romania. Enache is eighty-seven years old. His hair is completely white and he is blind. But he sits erect on a narrow bench, back to the wall, and his blue eyes dart about, as though still seeing, as he recounts the details of a massacre he witnessed in the summer of 1941, when he was sixteen, in the woods outside the village. The victims were Jewish civilians, the perpetrators Romanian soldiers. In October 2010, before he lost his sight, he led researchers to the scene of the killing. Opposite Enache, holding a tape recorder, sits Adrian Cioflâncă, the thirty-nine-year-old historian who directed the team that excavated the site.

The outskirts of Iași, a city of over a quarter of a million people, lie only five kilometres from Cuza Vodă, over the hills. But the journey Cioflâncă and I made to get here, along a winding dirt road, through chill November mist, was a trip back in time. Here, water is drawn from wells, in the yards of the tiny houses or by the roadside, and in each yard stands a wooden privy, like a sentry box. The vegetable gardens and orchards are bare in this season and the leaves have fallen from the vines. Geese waddle down to a muddy creek, across overgrazed common land. Landslides have taken bites from the hillsides.

Enache sits next to a brick stove. The stove is built into the wall, its sides plastered over and whitewashed. This is the winter room. The ceiling is so low you have to crouch a little as you enter. The windows are small, squinting. I sit to Enache's right, on the bench. On the bed, which is as long as the room is wide, sits Enache's wife. They have been married for sixty-eight years. Two of their five children are still alive. Standing by the door – there is no more room to sit – is Enache's daughter, Parascheva, an energetic cheerful woman in her fifties. She has her father's bright blue eyes.

'We finished the excavation, Mr Enache,' says Cioflâncă loudly, leaning forward. Enache's hearing is not so good these days. This is the first time that Cioflâncă and Enache have spoken in two years, since the completion of the excavation.

'You found them?'

'They're reburied now, in Iași. There's a monument.'

Enache nods and seems to disappear into himself for a moment.

'How many?'

'Thirty-six.'

'Thirty-six? There were many more than that. At least a hundred.'

'We only opened one grave.'

Cioflâncă knows Enache's story better than anyone. But he takes him through it again, hoping to elicit one more useful detail about this incident in one of the most terrible massacres of the war – the Iași pogrom, in which upward of ten thousand Jews were killed.

'Mr Enache, what time of the day was it when the soldiers took you? Was it morning?'

'Morning. Around ten o'clock.'

In 2010, when the excavation was underway, Enache recounted his story a number of times – to Cioflâncă, to a local journalist and to researchers from the Wiesel Institute. While none of those interviews could be described as exhaustive, and while Enache might not have been completely sober when giving them, the accounts are consistent with each other and with his retelling, now, in my presence.

Towards the end of the month of June, grazing a few cattle at the edge of Vulturi woods, several kilometres from his home, Enache was seized by

Romanian soldiers. War had just been declared by Germany and its allies, of which Romania was one, against the Soviet Union. The front lay only a few kilometres from Cuza Vodă. The soldiers were escorting a column of over a hundred Jewish prisoners. They might have suspected, wrongly, that Enache was Jewish. Or they might simply have wished to teach the boy a lesson for straying into a military area. They took him to a clearing in the forest, where he was held by two soldiers. He watched as the civilians were forced to dig their own graves. There were three pits. Those who had better clothes were made to undress and the clothing was piled beside the pit. The civilians were ordered, in groups of around ten, to sit with their backs to the soldiers, their legs dangling in the hole. The commander then asked for volunteers to perform the execution. Volunteers came forward. The civilians were shot from behind, from a distance of about three metres. Four prisoners were made to arrange the bodies in the pit so that more could fit, and a second group was lined up, facing the dead, and shot. Enache is unclear about how many times this happened. He speaks of people trying to escape, unsuccessfully. The area was completely ringed with soldiers.

Enache is not the easiest subject to interview. He has difficulty hearing. He is missing teeth, and mumbles. He has a heavy accent and uses regionalisms I am unfamiliar with. You do not always get a response to the question you ask. Cioflâncă does not get a clear answer as to why the soldiers might have thought, or claimed to believe, that Enache was Jewish. When asked where the executioners stood in relation to the victims – the grave is on a hillside – Enache is unable to remember or does not understand what he is being asked. But when Cioflâncă interrupts to ask if he remembers the rank of the commander, Enache replies after a brief pause:

'A Captain. I don't know his name.'

Enache saw over a hundred people killed, but he always remembers one victim in particular: 'There was one young woman. She had a child in her arms and she was begging for it to be spared. She was saying, "I beg you, let my child grow up, we've done nothing wrong, we're not animals." But it made no difference to them.'

Nobody speaks for a moment. Old Mrs Enache passes a hand over her face, whispers something I do not catch.

'After that, it was like I was turned to stone. I could have been killed myself. Can you imagine what that is like, looking into the grave, knowing they're aiming at your back? The ground shook with the cries of that that poor woman. And there were other people screaming. There was a terrible noise.'

When the pit was filled, the four men forced to arrange the corpses covered them with soil. Two pits were filled in this way. Finally, these four men were then lined up by a third pit and executed. The soldiers buried them.

The soldiers brought Enache to his village. Neighbours attested that he was a local Christian and he was freed.

'When I took the cows to graze after that, I was unable to pass by that place. I couldn't look at where they ended up, lifeless in the ground, and for no reason.'

The talk moves on to other subjects. Enache complains that Parascheva lets him have wine only on Thursdays and Sundays.

'It's for your health, father. Because of the medication.'

'At my age, it's about time I moved along,' he sputters, indignant.

'But at the appointed hour. Not from drinking.'

Parascheva's home is in Bucharest, eight hours away by train, where she has raised her family, but she spends alternate months in the village, looking after her elderly parents. When she is in Bucharest, it is the turn of her sister, who still lives in Cuza Vodă.

Our visit has lasted perhaps forty or fifty minutes when Enache begins to get agitated. He says he wants to go outside. It is time for us to leave. Cioflâncă takes a picture of Enache and he senses the flash. His eyes can still distinguish light from dark. As we get up to leave, Cioflâncă asks if he can photograph him outside, in what is left of the daylight.

Enache knows his way about his home and does not need to be guided. A wooden porch runs along the front of the house. It is a traditional dwelling made of mud and straw, plastered over and painted. Enache stands patiently on the porch and has his picture taken, alone and then with Cioflâncă. Beside Cioflâncă he looks very small. Then he says goodbye to us, raises his hand in a wave, and goes back indoors. Parascheva sees us to the gate. Cioflâncă and I get in the car and drive back along the winding dirt road, towards Iaşi.

The hillsides and woods around here are littered with unmarked graves; some contain a single body, others hundreds. Though many of these graves were soon forgotten, with the dispersal of the killers and any witnesses, in places such as Cuza Vodă an entire community knew and those who are still alive can tell you what they saw. But until very recently, nobody ever asked.

2

From the establishment of a Romanian state in the second half of the nineteenth century, antisemitism was enshrined in law. Jews faced restrictions on freedom of movement, ownership of property and the practising of professions. A ban on residence in small towns and rural areas meant that Jewish communities were frequently expelled and expropriated. Romanian independence from the Ottoman sphere of influence was recognized by the Congress of Berlin in 1878, in exchange for guarantees against religious discrimination. These commitments were soon reneged upon.

The treaties that followed the First World War produced a Greater Romania. The country doubled in size and population, and for the first time in history nearly all ethnic Romanians lived within a unitary state. At the same time, a third of the population of Greater Romania was not ethnically

Romanian. The new state was obliged by the treaties to grant citizenship to all its residents; Romania thus became the last state in Europe to grant citizenship to its Jews, who comprised slightly over 4 per cent of the population. By 1938, with antisemitism again on the rise, Jews were stripped of their citizenship. Three quarters of a million people – Europe's third largest Jewish population, after those of Poland and the Soviet Union – became aliens in their own land.

At the end of June 1940, Romania received a Soviet ultimatum for the cession of its territory between the rivers Prut and Dniester in the east (foreseen in a secret protocol of the Molotov–Ribbentrop pact between Hitler and Stalin in 1938). Three days were allowed for the withdrawal of Romanian troops. The only shots fired by the Romanian army as it hurried to get out of the path of the Soviets were in the direction of Jewish civilians. The first massacre took place in the locality of Mihoreni. Among the most useful sources for what happened to the Jews there, and elsewhere in Romania during the war, is *Cartea Neagră*, or *The Black Book*, based on testimonials and documentary sources gathered by Matatias Carp, a Romanian Jewish lawyer, and first published in 1947. On the orders of a Major Goilav, Carp writes, 'Soldiers arrested and tortured Shloime Weiner, his son Usher Weiner, his daughters Roza Weiner and Fani Zekler (the latter with a two-year-old infant in her arms). They were brought to Tureatca forest, where the crippled shoemaker Moscovici was already held, along with his wife and two children, as well as the wife of a certain Isac Moscovici with two little girls. They were lined up in front of a pit and shot.'

More than six hundred Jews are known to have been killed across the country over the following twelve months, though the frequent complicity of the police and the army make it certain that many incidents went unrecorded. The attacks were characterized by a spectacular degree of cruelty, including instances of people being thrown from trains, burned alive, or tortured prior to execution. Dismembered or eviscerated corpses were often left in public view. Old antisemitic narratives had gained new virulence by merging with the rhetoric emanating from the highest levels of the state. Stories invented in 1940 of retreating Romanian soldiers being insulted and attacked by jubilant Jews have endured to this day.

Territorial losses and the strengthening of German power across the continent accelerated the collapse of Romania's fragile political institutions. In September 1940 Romania became a 'National Legionary State', run by an alliance of the fascist Legionary movement (the 'Iron Guard') and the army under General Ion Antonescu. In November Romania officially allied itself with the Axis powers. A policy of 'Romanianization', intended to eliminate Jewish influence in the professions, public life and the economy, was applied. Jews were stripped of their assets, sometimes under a quasi-legal procedure, more often as a result of plain intimidation and robbery. In January, Antonescu himself expressed his dissatisfaction with the degree of disorder: 'They [members of the Iron Guard] go to the shops of the *jidani* [derogatory word for Jew] and take their stock, destroying both commerce and credit. At this rate, within two months we'll be witnessing an economic catastrophe. The factories will no longer supply their goods because the *jidani* shopkeepers aren't renewing their stock.'

Romania was at this time the second-largest oil producer in Europe, after the Soviet Union. By January 1941, with plans for Operation Barbarossa already being laid in Berlin, the Germans were counting upon this resource. Hitler had worries about the Iron Guard's potential to destabilize Romania economically and politically. Meeting on 14 January in Germany, he told Antonescu: 'You need to unyoke yourself from them [the Iron Guard]: in every militant movement there are fanatics who consider it their duty to destroy everything ... Such people need to be prevented from causing harm.' On 20 January, an Iron Guard attempt to wrest power from Antonescu became the occasion for a pogrom in Bucharest. Homes and businesses were attacked, and synagogues destroyed. Jews were beaten and tortured, and over

120 killed. The corpses of thirteen Jews murdered at an abattoir were hung from meat-hooks under the inscription 'Kosher meat'.

On 22 June, the Axis declared war on the Soviet Union, and the authorities immediately began to put into effect Antonescu's order to 'cleanse' the area between the rivers Siret and Prut in the east of the country by transferring all Jews between the ages of eighteen and sixty to a concentration camp in the interior. This order was quickly superseded by more general instructions to 'cleanse' the front of Jews. Iași, the largest Romanian city on the Soviet frontier, had a population slightly above 100,000. It was over one third Jewish, even before the influx of Jewish refugees from the surrounding countryside.

The panic and paranoia of war were exacerbated by the presence in Iași by Legionary elements – used as agitators by the Romanian secret services – who circulated rumours that Jews were signalling to the Soviet air force or staging attacks on the Romanian army. (Though Antonescu had suppressed the Iron Guard as an organization, many of its supporters were absorbed into the state.) The journal of the Jewish writer Mihail Sebastian, who lived in Bucharest, records on 24 June the appearance of propaganda posters in the capital that asked 'Who are the masters of Bolshevism?' above a cartoon of the guilty party: 'A Jew in a red gown, with side curls, skull cap, and beard, holding a hammer in one hand and a sickle in the other. Concealed beneath his coat are three Soviet soldiers. I have heard that the posters were put up by police sergeants.'

The war against the Soviet Union was to be a war against the Jews.

The Iași pogrom began on 28 June and continued over three days. Many of the victims died in their homes or in the street. Hundreds, or even thousands – reports vary, and it is impossible now to know – were shot down by Romanian police and German soldiers in a mass execution in the courtyard of the city's police headquarters, where they had been summoned, ostensibly, to receive documents guaranteeing their continued liberty. The killing at the police station took hours.

For days, in the absence of any plan for the burial of so many victims, the streets of Iași were littered with corpses. Bodies were buried in unmarked graves, left on rubbish tips or thrown into the river.

On 30 June two trains left Iași railway station with some 4,400 people packed onto goods wagons, daubed with slogans such as 'communist *jidani*' en route to an internment camp. The trains shuffled for days in the summer heat between local stations, and over 2,700 of the deportees died of suffocation or dehydration.

Had there remained any doubt that war had been declared against the Jews, an official communiqué, reprinted in all the Bucharest newspapers on 2 July, would have dispelled it: 'In recent days there have been incidents of hostile alien elements opposed to our interests opening fire on German and Romanian soldiers. Any attempt to repeat these vile attacks will be ruthlessly crushed. For each German or Romanian warrior, fifty Judeo-Communists will be executed.'

The Holocaust can be divided roughly into two periods. In the first, from the outbreak of the war in the east in June 1941 and into 1942, the advancing fascist armies exterminated Jewish civilians in mass shootings conducted over hours or even days, mostly by specialist mobile German death squads called *Einsatzgruppen*. The second stage involved the use of extermination camps and gas chambers, methods adopted for reasons of speed and efficiency. The second phase of the Holocaust is better documented than the first and has greater prominence in the contemporary consciousness, despite the fact that similar numbers of Jews died by bullet and by gas.

What Vasile Enache witnessed in Vulturi woods was the beginning of the first phase of the Holocaust; by the end of the year, across a front extending from the Baltic to the Black Sea, over a million Jews would be shot dead. Romanian troops were massacring Jewish civilians, of all ages and both sexes, from the first week of the war, and continued to do so in the weeks and months ahead, as they advanced north and east against the frantically retreating Soviet forces. They operated more or less spontaneously, in the absence of detailed instructions from above. Massacres committed by Germans, by contrast, tended to be orderly, planned events, often following the registration of the victims and their imprisonment in ghettos. We know that 33,771 people were shot by German troops on the outskirts of Kiev on the last two days of September 1941, but for the Iași massacre the margin of error is in the thousands; modern historians put the death toll between ten and fourteen thousand.

A report by an SS unit stationed in Romania, dated July 1941, complains about Romanian sloppiness: 'The Romanians act against Jews with no pre-conceived plan. Nobody would have anything to say about the very many executions of Jews if their technical preparation, as well as the way they are carried out, were not deficient. The Romanians leave executed people to lie where they fall, without burying them. Einsatzcommando has demanded that the Romanian police proceed in a more orderly fashion in this respect.'

Over 300,000 Romanian Jews would die in the Holocaust. In addition, more than 100,000 Soviet Jews would die in Transnistria, the swathe of Ukraine between the Dniester and the Bug that was placed under Romanian wartime administration.

3

I first met Adrian Cioflâncă in the autumn of 2012, having learned of his role in the excavation of the mass grave at Vulturi woods. I was curious to hear how he had first become aware of the Iași pogrom, and he told me that, as an adolescent, he had heard an account of an incident in that city when Romanian soldiers took revenge on some Jews who had attacked them. Although information about the massacre had reached the Jewish community in Bucharest within weeks – Mihail Sebastian's diary contains references to the death trains and the slaughter at the police station – the propaganda versions of events given by the Antonescu regime at the time have retained currency.

Romanian communism, as nationalist as it was socialist, did not discuss anything that might complicate the story of Romanian national destiny, and that included mention of the genocide committed in the nation's name. Even in the 1990s, school and university history courses ended with the outbreak of war in 1940. When socialism was officially ditched, the nationalist residue remained. 'I went on to study history in Iaşi myself in the 1990s and never learned about the pogrom in that city,' Cioflâncă told me. 'In the '90s, contemporary history was taboo, an area that couldn't be properly investigated. And there was the dominance of nationalist "party" historians from the '60s, '70s and '80s who wrote ideological books. You had nowhere to find out about the war. I didn't learn about the pogrom until about ten years ago, when I was working for a newspaper in Iaşi and they published a series of eyewitness accounts.'

Our discussion was taking place at Cioflâncă's office at the headquarters of the National Council for the Study of the Archives of the Securitate, or CNSAS. The CNSAS was established in 1999 in order to put in the public domain the hoard of documents amassed by the Securitate – Romania's internal security apparatus – under communism, including records from military courts. It is one of the archives that Cioflâncă has used to begin the laborious task of building a database of victims of the Iaşi pogrom.

In 1946, a tribunal was instigated to examine war crimes by the Antonescu regime. Cases were followed up by civilian and military courts and resulted in 187 convictions. By 1959, hundreds more trials had resulted in convictions. The major massacres, such as those in Iaşi and in Odessa (where the Romanian army massacred 23,000 Jews), were given particular attention, though a number of cases involving small numbers of victims were also tried. In some cases, says Cioflâncă, the investigations of the events were thorough, while in others they were superficial and propagandistic. Most of the killings were carried out by small units of the Romanian army which for reasons of secrecy did not issue written orders, so no documentary evidence of their acts remains. This explains how a massacre in a rural area, such as that at Vulturi, could go unregistered at the official level.

The trials were carried out in an atmosphere of terror by a nascent Stalinist state set on eliminating ideological opponents of every hue. There was an accent upon the criminal nature of the fascist regime, but – as in the Soviet Union – a reluctance to examine the killing of Jews as a distinct phenomenon. Then, in the 1960s, Romania's communist regime became increasingly nationalistic, and the Holocaust remained a taboo subject for the quarter century of Ceaușescu's rule. Romania's Holocaust was buried in silence.

Impending EU membership put pressure on the Romanian government to acknowledge the country's role in the Holocaust. In 2004, the country's leaders participated for the first time in remembrance ceremonies, a monument to Holocaust victims was erected in Bucharest and the Elie Wiesel National Institute for Holocaust Research was established, under the Ministry of Culture. Romania joined the EU in 2007 and the Holocaust now figures in school textbooks, but only as part of an optional course; students can still leave school without ever hearing of the mass killing of Romanian Jews.

In the spring of 2010, Adrian Cioflâncă (who had since 2005 been teaching a master's degree course in Jewish history at Iași University) was contracted by the Wiesel Institute to compile an oral history of a cluster of villages north of the city, including Cuza Vodă. By collating local recollections with the patchy archival evidence, it was hoped he could locate at least one of the unmarked graves reputed to be in the locality.

The villagers were able to provide Cioflâncă with unexpectedly detailed information. Older people in Cuza Vodă and other villages told of groups of between twenty and eighty Jews passing in columns along the roads over several weeks in the summer of 1941, escorted by Romanian troops. The locals sometimes recognized individual prisoners, and they remembered the civilians being taken into Vulturi and other woods. Screams and the sound of automatic gunfire would be heard. A local man, Stefan Clim from the village of Carlig, was engaged by the army to sell the victims' clothes, and witnesses remembered seeing him transporting them by cart. (Clim is believed to have died in hospital in 1945.) After the war, when the forests were demilitarized, the villagers came across the graves. One site in Vulturi woods, in a small valley called Climoaiei, was even known locally as 'the grave of the Jews' and a preliminary investigation by archaeologists from Iaşi University indicated an area where the ground had been disturbed. When Cioflâncă asked locals why they had never before spoken about the graves in the woods, they responded that nobody had ever asked them.

Since the excavation in September 1945 of mass graves some three kilometres from Vulturi – a place called Stânca Roznoveanu – there had never been any serious effort by the Romanian authorities to physically investigate the sites of wartime massacres. At Stânca Roznoveanu, 311 bodies were recovered from three pits. Military documents had acknowledged the killing there of forty people – 'which warns us', Cioflâncă told me, 'that documents aren't final evidence for any serious investigation'.

The reports of 'the grave of the Jews' in Vulturi were significant because there was no documentary evidence of a massacre there. It was an opportunity, however small or apparently symbolic, to bring to light events previously unrecorded or officially suppressed.

'What we do know is that the the same regiment implicated in the Stânca Roznoveanu massacre and others in the area – the 6th Vânători – also had jurisdiction over the woods at Vulturi,' Cioflâncă told me. 'It was an elite unit on a mission to "cleanse" the area just behind the front.'

The Vulturi grave would have been difficult to locate without local help. The woodland can be crossed in under an hour by foot, but it covers a series of small valleys, from which radiate even smaller ridges and gullies that look identical to the untrained eye. The area was militarized during the war and for a time was the front line. The ground has been dug over and banked up in many places and surveys with metal detectors indicate numerous areas with concentrations of spent ammunition.

And then it was discovered that an eyewitness to the killing at Vulturi was living in Cuza Vodă. On a wet autumn day in 2010, Adrian Cioflâncă, accompanied by the archaeologist Neculai Bolohan, called to the home of Vasile Enache. They explained that they wished him to confirm the massacre site before they began excavating.

Enache was confused. 'Historical research? Archaeological survey? What's that?' he asked.

Vasile Enache had always lived in Cuza Vodă and had never travelled far from it. He had spent most of his adult life under one of Europe's most repressive and paranoid communist dictatorships, and the authorities had never shown any interest in the massacre he had witnessed. So he could not understand why, after so many years, somebody wanted to escort him back to Vulturi woods so that he could point to the place where he had seen people shot.

The edge of Vulturi woods is less than two kilometres from Vasile Enache's home, across fields and hills. But the journey by road is a circuitous eight kilometres, and the last section is up a steep and rutted forestry road that deteriorates in wet weather.

'We got stuck in the mud,' Cioflâncă told me. 'It had started raining and we were wearing very brightly coloured raincoats, one red, one blue. We looked kind of like a special operations squad. And it was like in the films. We got out of the jeep, and he asked us to turn around so he could relieve himself. Then he took off, running through the woods. The more we ran after him, shouting, "Come back, nothing's going to happen", the faster he went, saying "Don't kill me! Leave me alone!" If someone had come along and seen us chasing this old man … We had to let him go.'

Enache returned home by foot, cross-country.

'He couldn't understand, either then or later, what we were doing there,' says Cioflâncă. 'We were Jews who'd come for revenge, that was his explanation.'

The researchers let several days elapse before approaching Enache again. This time they went in the company of a local, and after having spoken with his daughter, Parascheva, who managed to convince him that the researchers meant no harm. Parascheva also instructed the researchers to walk ahead of her father when visiting the site.

'We approached very slowly,' says Cioflâncă, 'and he pointed out the area where the preliminary survey already suggested the grave was.'

The Wiesel Institute directed Cioflâncă and his team from Iaşi University to carry out an excavation. The dig began on 27 October 2010.

'There's a grave in Valea Climoaiei, I know that,' said Enache, speaking to a local journalist as the excavation commenced. 'And someone wants to dig them up, even if they're just bones now. But maybe there are people alive now who have relatives or loved ones who were thrown in those holes. So I went back in the woods, a second time, to show them where it was. I went with a man from Cârlig, to be sure nobody did us any harm.'

4

The public prosecutor was informed of the excavation on the day it began. With a living eyewitness to the massacre, Vulturi had the peculiar status of being both an archaeological investigation and a crime scene.

Initially, the authorities showed little interest. They instructed the researchers to put any human remains in bags and let them know when they were finished. 'Which was very good,' Cioflâncă said, 'because it meant we were able to work without pressure from the media and the authorities, who would have taken over if they'd been involved. … we decided to release the information in a controlled way.'

The skeletons unearthed included those of children. Remnants of clothing and personal effects were found, including buttons, a belt buckle, the sole of a woman's shoe and a lady's watch. The ammunition found was Romanian army issue and had left the factory in 1939 and 1940. Even without Enache's testimony, everything pointed to the killing of civilians by the Romanian army. Despite this, the Chief Public Prosecutor in Iaşi, Cornelia Prisăcariu, made the following statement:

> I want to stress that at this point in time we don't know if we are deal-ing with the remains of civilians or Romanian troops. It's possible too that they are Russian or German soldiers. The area was the front line in World War II. At this point, we can't affirm that we're dealing with the Jewish population, or comment on statements that it is Jews that have really been found there … Opinions voiced at present concern-ing these remains have no scientific basis. Statements by witnesses need to be backed up by scientific proof. In the case before us, we're dealing with memories from childhood, concerning things that hap-pened sixty or seventy years ago.

Notwithstanding the Chief Public Prosecutor's remarks, the evidence for Romanian Army involvement in the killing was sufficient for the case to be immediately turned over to the Military Prosecutor. The military authorities allowed part of the original research team to remain in place, and the mili-tary were furnished with the documentary evidence that provided the context for the crime.

The excavation continued for another two weeks, through November, under pressure to finish before winter set in. A rabbinical group protested that the disturbance of the remains was in contravention of Jewish tradition. But the site was now that of a criminal investigation, and this trumped the religious objections.

By the end of November all the skeletons had been removed from the grave and placed in individual bags. There were also several bags of 'unattributed' bones. Laboratory analysis determined that the remains came from thirty-six individuals: twelve children, nine women and fifteen men. The oldest victim was perhaps eighty years of age. The youngest was a child of two or three.

There are witness reports and documentary evidence of other massacre sites elsewhere in the region, but Cioflâncă has not been able to secure permission and funding to conduct further excavations. 'Only recently, I was looking at the cases of captured Romanian soldiers who were convicted of war crimes, many of them from the regiment we've incriminated in the Vulturi massacre, the 6th Vânători,' says Cioflâncă. 'We have the charge sheets of Romanian prisoners who were sent home from the Soviet Union in 1955, and they're very valuable to historians, because they show that there were numerous small massacres of this type – I mean, of tens or even hundreds of people – which we've never known about. We're only finding out today that there were people arrested, tried and who served long sentences for these crimes.'

5

The historiography of the Holocaust has, naturally, emphasized the leading role of Germany. This has been facilitated by the accessibility and comprehensiveness of German archives, and by German willingness to confront the past. In contrast, a number of the post-war communist states of eastern Europe adopted, to varying degrees, policies of what would now be called

Holocaust denial; archival material and the testimony of witnesses was neglected or suppressed. The Romanian and Soviet states in particular took care not to damage nationalist narratives with stories of collaboration. In the areas where most of Europe's Jews lived and died, they have been most readily forgotten. And the old nationalist historical narratives, having never been challenged, have retained their potency.

On 4 April 2011, the remains of the victims of the Vulturi massacre were reinterred at the Jewish cemetery in Iaşi. Eleven months later, on 5 March 2012, Dan Şova, the thirty-nine-year-old spokesman for the Party of Social Democracy (PSD), gave an interview on television. 'On Romanian territory, no Jews were made to suffer,' said Şova, 'and this is thanks to Antonescu.' He went on to refer specifically to the Iaşi pogrom: 'Unfortunately, twenty-three or -four Romanian citizens of Jewish origin were killed by German soldiers … Romanians were not involved in the massacre in Iaşi. This is a historical fact.'

Though a lawyer by profession, Dan Şova graduated with a degree in History from Bucharest University in 2001. His party, the PSD, is not a fringe grouping. It is Romania's largest political party. The day after the interview, PSD leader Victor Ponta relieved Şova of his responsibilities as party spokesman and stated that as a result of his 'enormous gaffe' Şova would be sent on a trip to the Holocaust Memorial Museum in Washington, DC.

In his first statements after his 'gaffe', Şova regretted that his comments had been 'misunderstood'. He had not meant to deny Romanian involvement in the Holocaust, he claimed, and only wanted to say that the Romanian people had never desired such a thing, which had occurred only due to the country being pushed into an alliance with Nazi Germany.

It soon became clear to the young politician that historically inaccurate equivocation on the subject of the Holocaust would cripple his career in a party that cherishes its EU photo opportunities. In his subsequent public statements, including an open letter to the Israeli ambassador, he managed to say all the right things. He has not stopped apologizing since.

Late in 2012, when I first began to research the Iași massacre and the excavation at Vulturi, I contacted the historian Radu Ioanid, the author of the most authoritative work on the Holocaust in Romania, *Evreii sub Regimul Antonescu* (an English version was published as *The Holocaust in Romania*). Ioanid directs the International Archival Division at the Holocaust Memorial Museum in Washington, DC, and in that role he had been been pressing since 2002 for the mass graves around Iași to be located and examined. In 2010, he directed efforts to assemble the team that conducted the excavation at Vulturi. Ioanid was on a brief visit to Romania and I was keen to meet him, both to talk about Vulturi and to find out if Șova had actually paid an educational visit to the museum.

Ioanid described receiving a telephone call from Victor Ponta, the PSD leader: 'Ponta called me on the phone. He asked me if I'd take Șova. I told him anyone was free to visit the museum, he didn't need special permission. So he came for three days. I had someone assist him with the archives, particularly the documents and photographs from the Iași pogrom. When he was finished he sat down with me in my office and I asked him how he had come to make such an insane affirmation. He told me something about doing history under Buzatu.'

Gheorghe Buzatu, a mainstream nationalist historian during the communist period, continued lecturing, writing and publishing after the overthrow of Ceaușescu, and represented Iași as Senator for the far-right Greater Romania Party from 2000 to 2004. In his published works, Buzatu cited as an academic authority David Irving, the British Holocaust-denier. Buzatu did not become marginalized in academic circles in Romania until after 2004, when Romania's impending membership of the EU produced the state's first official acknowledgment of Romanian involvement in the Holocaust.

Ioanid and I were sitting on a first-floor balcony of the Bucharest Hilton, overlooking a stretch of downtown Bucharest that could be read as a summary of a couple of centuries of Romanian history. We could see the Royal

Palace (now an art museum), the imposing relic of a royal family imported, Balkan-style, in the nineteenth century; the last king, Carol II, had tried to become dictator in 1938, only to be sidelined by the fascists and finally deposed by the communists. Across the street from the Royal Palace was the blocky Soviet-style headquarters of the Communist Party of Romania (today the Interior Ministry), from the balcony of which Ceaușescu had given his last speech. With the crowd turning on him, he made his escape from the roof by helicopter, only to be captured and shot three days later. The Communist Party disbanded itself or, some might say, renamed itself and entered the democratic era as the National Salvation Front. The Front soon split into factions, of which the most successful today is Șova's party, the PSD. Several months after Șova's trip to Washington, the PSD found itself in government. Victor Ponta became prime minister, and appointed Dan Șova as Minister for Liaison with Parliament.

Asked about Șova's visit to Washington, Ioanid shrugged. 'He made a mistake, he acknowledged it. I don't think you should be hounded for a mistake.' Was Șova really repentant, I wondered, or just going through the motions? Another shrug, suggesting it did not matter terribly much. 'He's a politician,' said Ioanid. 'Time will tell.'

Certainly, when I went back later to examine the statements on Șova's blog, it was the politician I saw. On National Holocaust Remembrance Day (9 October) Minister Șova posted a statement that reads like a copy-paste pastiche of what public figures say on such occasions ('... the great tragedy of the Holocaust ... our duty to the memory of those who perished ... that it may never happen again'). Șova went on declare his involvement in a number of initiatives 'to transmit to the younger generations the lessons of history which we were not able to learn in school and which are absolutely necessary for a civilized country'.

Minister Șova does not offer to explain how he had failed, in the twenty-two years since the fall of communism, to hear about the Romanian

Holocaust. It is a pity, because his explanation might tell us something important about contemporary Romania. It might tell us something about a virulent strain of Romanian nationalism that preceded communism, thrived within it, and has outlived it. As it is, all we have learned is how easy it is, even within the EU, to go from being a Holocaust denier to being a government minister. In a matter of months.

6

In November 2012, I took a train from Bucharest, where I live, to the city of Iași, where I was to meet up with Adrian Cioflâncă for our visit to Vasile Enache in Cuza Vodă. I arrived shortly before midnight and walked through cold and almost deserted streets to my hotel.

The next day, I walked around, trying to get a sense of a city I knew only from books. Iași was the capital of the principality of Moldova, and after the principalities of Moldova and Wallachia united in 1859 the city was briefly, with Bucharest, joint capital of the new entity. At that time, Iași rivalled Bucharest in size and cultural prestige. Something of old Iași remains today, in the form of some especially grand civic architecture, such as the Palace of Culture, and in the very beautiful Church of the Three Kings, and in the university. It is perhaps because of these echoes of a grand past that today the city feels oddly shrunken, depleted, as though there is insufficient human energy to animate what is left. New suburbs were built during the decades after the war, but they were built on nothing very solid, and the population has declined by nearly a quarter since the fall of communism. Iași is now a provincial backwater. Recovery from the failures of communism has not been helped by the city's location, in the depressed east of the country, on the border with what was the Soviet Union, now that Romania's trade is geared decisively westward. But I couldn't help thinking of the proportion of the city's population in 1941 that was Jewish. In this part of Europe, from the Baltic to the Black Sea, it is not possible to talk of the growth of cities and urban institutions, or the development of commerce and the arts, without talking of the Jews. They Jewish people were part of what once linked Europe together, before civilization turned on itself, murderously, and destroyed its own fabric.

If you are especially interested, you can examine the traces of Jewish life in Iași: the silent walls of the main synagogue, or the little monument that marks the location of what was once a Yiddish theatre (the world's first). Along with being one of Romania's most important Jewish centres, Iași was also the cradle of its most violent antisemitic political movements including, finally and decisively, the Iron Guard. In judging the decline of Iași, it could be argued that the city has had an unfortunate history. It could be argued just as easily that Iași did its best to destroy itself, and that this happened over a few bloody days in the early summer of 1941.

The day before I visited Cuza Vodă and heard Vasile Enache's story, I went to the Jewish cemetery in Iași. The cemetery is on a hillside at the edge of the city, and as you climb the road to its gates the city spreads out below you. A pack of barking, snarling dogs appeared as I approached the entrance. They had surrounded me and were getting dangerous by the time an old woman appeared from the dilapidated gate lodge and called them off. I told her I had come to see the monument for the people who had died in Vulturi wood. She showed me the way, muttered something about a donation. I had no kippa and she had none to lend me and did not seem to care about the breach of protocol. I kept my hood up instead, and we walked to the monument, eight or ten dogs at our heels. 'They won't do anything,' the old woman said, irritated at my nervousness. 'We don't have guards here. They do the job.'

The monument is a large piece of black marble. The inscription states that it marks the place of rest of reinterred victims of the Antonescu regime, and gives the place and month of their death. Along the ground in front of the headstone is a long slab with a row of thirty-six identical horizontal stones upon it, one for each of the anonymous victims. It has not been possible to identify any of them, nor even to establish whether they were from Iași itself or from an outlying town or village.

The monument for the victims of the Vulturi massacre stands near an older mass grave and monument to the victims of the Iași pogrom. The rows of sarcophogi in front of the monument are symbolic, because these dead too are anonymous.

On 20 June 1941, a full week before the start of the pogrom, the head of a forced-labour battalion comprising 110 young Jewish men received an order to begin digging, as a matter of urgency, two pits at the Jewish cemetery. The pits were completed by 26 June and measured thirty and fifteen metres in length respectively. They were two metres deep and two metres wide. At least 254 of the victims of the mass shooting at the police headquarters of 29 June were buried here. The bodies were transported in two trucks and twenty-four carts, over two days. The dead were buried with the dying. Walking over to read the inscription, I wandered too far from the old woman. The dogs decided to attack, bounding towards me over the tops of sarcophogi. The biggest dog, barking and snarling, knocked over a candle in its holder. It rolled off the top of the sarcophagus, onto the grass by my feet. The old woman came running, shouting at the dogs. I picked the candle up and replaced it. Weeds and young trees were coming through the cracks in the monument and beyond it stretched the city of Iași. A string of little Israeli flags draped the monument, incongruous, like bunting. They fluttered in the cold breeze. Did many visitors come from Israel? I asked the old woman. 'Oh yes, in the summer. Now isn't the season.'

No, it was not the season, and we walked back towards the gate, past older stones inscribed in Hebrew characters, and the graveyard ran in grassy alleys up the hillside. One big tree had fallen between the rows. The graveyard extended over twenty-six hectares, said the old woman. I would have liked to walk it alone, and to take my time, but that was impossible. More dogs appeared. There might have been twenty of them. What do you feed them? I asked the old woman. She shrugged. 'Whatever I have. Bones.' We reached the gate, where the tombstones alternated with kennels hammered together out of bits of plywood, and I gave the old woman some money.

Notes on Bowie

BRIAN DILLON

'For nearly ten minutes he stood there, motionless, with parted lips, and eyes strangely bright. He was dimly conscious that entirely fresh influences were at work within him. Yet they seemed to have come really from himself.'

— Oscar Wilde, *The Picture of Dorian Gray* (1890)

'Get out of my mind, all of you!'

— David Bowie, in *The Man Who Fell to Earth* (1976)

1

I'm enthralled and embarrassed by him in ways that are probably possible only when you have loved too much and too soon. Not only am I mystified on discovering that some people my age or a little older are quite indifferent to David Bowie; I also feel much the same ache and anger when I hear him disparaged as I did thirty years ago. While I was taking notes for this essay a friend pointed to a newspaper article: a tedious columnist was claiming that, all brilliance and invention aside, Bowie has never written a song that truly moved anyone, still less consoled them in the wake, let's say, of a bereavement. Surely this is true, said my friend. Really? You have no idea, I think – none.

And yet: the embarrassment. Not so much at the unengaging records that followed his decade or so of genius and are easily ignored, nor the silliness of this or that image or hubristic acting project. I'm embarrassed instead at a certain brittle grandiloquence, at the inflated thoughts he makes me think. Things like: in or around the summer of 1981, my consciousness changed for good. Or: David Bowie invented me, and he may well have invented you. And the questions he makes me ask, such as this: how much of who you are is still in thrall to images and ideas planted decades ago by someone who was not even sure who or what *he* wanted to be? Someone whose influence you shared with millions? Exaggerated, sentimental, adolescent questions. Middle-aged ones, too.

2

David Jones was born in Brixton and grew up mostly in Bromley, Kent. (I find it hard to write simple facts about him. I have at this point read so many awful Bowie biographies that even typing that sentence feels like it might do bad things to my prose.) His mother had been a cinema usherette; his father, having squandered an inheritance of £3,000 in abortive efforts to set himself up as a show-business impresario, had settled into a job organizing fundraising entertainments for Barnardo's children's homes. When David was about ten years old his father took him to meet Tommy Steele, the alarmingly toothy all-round entertainer whose passing facial resemblance to Bowie still looks in retrospect like an awful warning as to the sort of artist he might have become. Except: there is more, still, of Tommy Steele and a host of other middle-of-the-road actors and singers, more of the straight entertainer's eagerness to please, in Bowie's career and persona than he or I or the curators of a vast Bowie exhibition at the Victoria and Albert Museum have cared to admit.

3

'If you could look like anybody in the world?' Still, thirty and more years after the question first occurred to me – still, no contest.

4

I've been staring at David Bowie's face now for quite some time. It's a cliché regarding the ubiquity of certain faces, but I feel as if I know its planes, moods and textures as well as if not better than the faces of people I love. I mean, people I love more than I love David Bowie. I've seen this face looking practisedly aloof: it's the expression you likely picture when you think of David Bowie – if you think of David Bowie. I've watched it crack into a repertoire of no less calculated demeanours: a hollow and paranoid cyborg glare beloved of bad Bowie impersonators; a sidelong darting look of surprise that suggests the subject's jittery mind has been momentarily engaged by an otherwise dull interlocutor; the sort of faintly embarrassing lost-in-music pout that singers of his generation all adopt on stage at the moment the lead guitarist really cuts loose.

There's an array too of apparently spontaneous grins: a raptorial, triumphant version mid-performance; a naive variant, soon to be controlled, in early publicity photos; the smile that accompanies the slightly panicked charm Bowie deploys in interviews and which conjures, whether he knows it or not, the essence of 1960s showbiz-lad-on-the-make. (Has there ever been an interviewee quite so *charming* as David Bowie? You're as likely to spot this smile and the boyish chat that goes with it in interviews from a decade ago as in, say, a late-1970s exchange with Janet Street Porter as he's about to go on stage – 'I've got a show to do! Coming?' – or even in the midst of cocaine paranoia.) Also, an awkward sneer that seems almost painfully to distort a face whose habitual tendency, so its owner would have us believe, is towards a properly iconic repose. It's an expression that makes me think of Kenneth Tynan writing about Noël Coward: a man with a face like 'an appalled monolith'.

Here is one expression that I have not seen repeated. The film clip is just seconds long, and comes from some time in the late 1970s; it might even have been shot in Berlin, where he had fled after a famously excessive and exhausting period in Los Angeles. Exhausting and excessive personally, that is. There are no ups and downs artistically for Bowie in the 1970s, just astonishing consistency of achievement amid those frequent reinventions, until at decade's end it all stops, or near enough. But that is to get ahead of ourselves. It's night and Bowie is out with a small retinue when he is spotted and the crowd gets too close for comfort. A figure that might be a man or a woman lunges forward and kisses him. Bowie grins and staggers a little and seems to go limp, gazes into the middle distance with a docile look and simply lets it all happen. Addressing himself now to the camera he strikes a perfect because entirely passive pose, and his face is the face of any instance of lazy, angelic cool you care to mention: from Bacall, Capote and Brando to the opiated half-presence of Brian Jones or Marianne Faithfull. Bowie, of course, haloed here in black and white, knows all of this and more: he sees us seeing the references. He's managed in a split second to parlay the moment his charisma cracks into something louche, funny, seductive, self-conscious and consequently (almost touchingly) foolish.

5

The V&A began trailing its exhibition last year, which only made him seem more remote. And then he was back: back from the near-dead – heart attack, a few guest appearances on other people's stages, apparent retirement – to sing

'Walking the Dead', conjuring the ghosts of his Berlin past, as if we hadn't heard from him since 1978. (Lyrically, at least; the music was something else, something less.) Then another single, and a video: Bowie playing at suburban dread with his doppelgänger Tilda Swinton – among other things a neat way of reminding us of his ambiguous and covetable looks. And a third single, courting in the video the fury of Catholic PR folk in the mock-priestly company of Gary Oldman.

All of this seemed to me perfectly fine. I began to look forward to the exhibition. But listen to the album? It may yet happen. I've dipped in, and discovered him executing, not for the first time, a more than passable imitation of recent Scott Walker: a singer he's admired, and at some level hoped to be, since the mid 1960s. Walker really is now the singer Bowie could have been – vanished from the mainstream, pursuing sonic and vocal experiments of amazing audacity at the end of his seventh decade, to uniformly glowing reviews – had he only elected to stop and think thirty years ago.

6

The V&A show opened in March. When I arrived in Kensington one midweek morning in June, there were at least a hundred people queueing before the show opened. Bowie allowed access, presumably not unfettered, to his personal archive, which turns out to be huge. Ever the enthusiast to the point of unabashed geekiness when it comes to his earliest influences, he has also been collecting assiduously, since the 1960s, the ephemera generated by his own career: felt-tip lyrics, diaries ('Lots of prospects. Am happy.'), correspondence, set lists, a good-luck telegram from Elvis at the start of a tour in 1976, notes from a suit fitting in 1972 (waist: twenty-six-and-a-half inches), a tissue blotted with his own lipstick, Brian Eno's analogue synthesizer as deployed on the three Berlin albums, countless pristine costumes hung on mannequins, some of which have Bowie's face, or rather the face of a life mask made in the mid 1970s, which is also in the show. The exhibition is called *David Bowie Is*: a faintly embarrassing title that allows the curators and museum marketeers to append various words and phrases: 'David Bowie is … blowing our minds … gazing a gazely stare … dressed from head to toe … content.' The one thing it never tells us is the most obvious: David Bowie is a collector.

Though it's not quite chronological – there are too many examples of futurist projection, knowing self-quotation and frank nostalgia in Bowie's career for a strict narrative arc to make sense – the exhibition begins with an origin myth of sorts: the London boy exiled early to the suburbs, there to dream of his return to the city via the sounds and images of a borrowed American culture. So here is one of David Jones's first guitars, the white plastic saxophone his parents bought him, his framed publicity photo of Little Richard. And a few years later: the teenager playing sax with, then fronting, a succession of quite hopeless bands: the Konrads, the King Bees, the Lower Third, the Manish Boys, the Buzz. There are concert tickets and press releases, hints already of the image he wants to project: the teenage reader of Camus, Pinter, Behan, Wilde. But there's some disparity still between the character and the records. The museum's brilliantly designed audio guide, which is cued with extreme precision to one's physical place in the gallery and proximity to specific exhibits, is not playing songs from Bowie's pre-fame years: songs with overly chirpy vocals and naively aspirant lyrics about drugs and sex and being young in London. Instead my headphones deliver echoey fragments of the achieved performer and persona to come, just around the corner: 'There's a starman …'

The first time I cried at the David Bowie exhibition: in the second gallery space there was a large vitrine, and in this vitrine the tight jumpsuit Bowie wore to perform 'Starman' on *Top of the Pops* on 5 July 1972, and behind it a more-than-life-size screen on which during that performance Bowie, grinning, draped an arm around his guitarist Mick Ronson, just as they reached the chorus. It's a moment that Bowie fans who were in their teens at the time recall with extreme fondness: a slow detonation of glamour and sex and strangeness in living rooms across the UK (and parts of Ireland too, I suppose, though likely in black and white). I was three years old, and I didn't see this footage until I was in my mid teens – such things were rarely repeated or excerpted before then. So why these tears?

I've listened to all the 1970s records again, especially those (at least half of them) that I never owned or never heard in their entirety as a child or a teenager. And they are all extraordinary: filled with melodies and textures and small miracles of phrasing – this last always for me, at least in Bowie's case, more important than lyrical import or even skill – that still surprise, still fascinate. But more frequently I've been poring online – such now is the hunt-and-peck modus of middle-aged nostalgia – over certain performances, interesting myself in those moments when Bowie seems on the cusp of one of his celebrated self-inventions, when it appears he has pushed a style as far as it will bear and you can see, or fancy that you can see, how it might be dispensed with. Thus Bowie, six months before his first hit, practising attitudes of Ziggy-like self-awareness in a 1969 promo film for 'Let Me Sleep Beside You' – the first of his records to be produced by Tony Visconti, the first of his records to really sound like a David Bowie record. Or in 1973, live on *Top of the Pops* in Ziggy's imperial phase, turning 'The Jean Genie' into a blaring affront to the Rolling Stones, whom he seemed for a time intent on outstripping. (Though for once not musically: the riff is Muddy Waters via the Yardbirds.) Or pushing 'Space Oddity' an octave higher than the original record into even more airless precincts of loneliness and paranoia – this in 1979, on of all things *The Kenny Everett Show* – as if he knows that the next task is a stark appraisal of the preceding decade and the place it has deposited him. I doubt anybody, even Bowie, had watched all of these performances until the advent of YouTube; before that they survived mostly as daydreams and partial memories.

9

Some time during my researches word went around among artists I know that Bowie is commissioning new videos to go with his old songs. My heart sank a little at the news – but who would say no to such an invitation? One lesson of the V&A exhibition is that he has not only been a collector, but an assiduous curator of his own career. Not so much in the inevitable repackaging of greatest hits, where he has more than once lost control of sub-par releases and embarrassing juvenilia, but rather in the songs themselves, in inflections of vocal delivery that recall tracks from decades past, or in radically altered performances of old songs that announce a new direction. Perhaps in the last analysis Bowie's profoundest obsession has been not with reinvention, as his admirers like to say, or with image, as detractors have it, but with time and its passing, with more or less avowed expressions of where he has been and what it might be made to mean now.

But none of this is yet *a propos* in the matter of Bowie and me. How to reconstruct the moment I fell for his image, then his music, and with them the very idea of Bowie: the sense that just invoking his name was still, in the early 1980s, an act of quite risky self-positioning? For a start, I found him late. I have no memory at all of Bowie in the 1970s, let alone the early glam-rock phase. (One of my first memories is of asking my father one Saturday evening who the shiny hairy person on TV was, and being told 'Gary Glitter'. I've always hoped he was wrong, that it was if not Bowie, who seems unlikely, it was at least Marc Bolan.) By the end of the decade, when I was paying attention, Bowie was an intermittent presence on the kind of television I'd have seen, so that it's quite possible I simply missed him. The gap has been filled by so much footage since, of which more below, that at times I can cathect as much retrospective wonder and desire into his best performances as any sparkling or hennaed teen of the time.

Here is the moment – my inaugural Bowie moment. It is the last year of national school: a very bad year as I recall for extremes of violence from classmates and teachers. (The summer term will end with my being kicked in the face at the school gates.) So my stomach churns one afternoon when, sitting two seats from the back of the classroom, I'm repeatedly prodded in the ribs by the boy behind me. He carries on hissing my name until finally I turn. For once I'm wrong about his intentions, because now he's jabbing at his own chest: 'See that, Dillon?'

I stare at the large badge he's wearing. 'Yeah ...'

Then a question. 'Is that a man or a woman?'

This might have been a test: one of those provoking challenges that in a suburban Dublin playground of the usual viciousness had lately progressed to quite gnomic questions. Certain of my classmates were now in the habit, once they had got you against a wall or surrounded on the bus early in the morning, of asking pointedly: 'Mod or ska?' Or more mysteriously: 'Are you a mod or a ska?' I think I knew even then that the use of the article in the latter case was idiosyncratic at best: ska was surely a type of music and not an identity in itself, even if you could easily spot its adherents in their Harrington jackets, as opposed to parkas. Still, subcultural semantics were not the reason I'd answered the question as I did one morning at the bus stop: 'Neither – I'm a human being!' My tormenters could not restrain their hilarity, nor their fists. I'm pretty sure that my smug, taunting answer was not unconsidered; like many a sensitive prepubescent I nursed not only a fear of, but a real fury and contempt towards, the nascent factional allegiances of adolescence. It seemed genuinely pathetic to me to have so defined yourself by something as crude as your taste in pop music (not to mention outerwear) that you'd resort to violence in the face of the wrong answer, or no answer at all. I recall despising the category of the teenager *tout court*, and resolving never to become one.

'Is that a man or a woman, Dillon?' The question was louder now; the teacher must have been out of the room, or the exchange would not have continued like this.

I was sure I was about to be punched, or the rest of the class invited to join in my torment. 'I don't know!'

He grinned triumphantly, stopped thrusting the badge in my face. 'Exactly!' And why, exactly? 'Because that's David Bowie!'

What I'd been looking at all this while was a close portrait shot of a person in a wide-brimmed hat – later I'd learn the word 'fedora' – pulled down at one side over a pair of large sunglasses. The photograph was almost half a decade old: an age in Bowie time, and schoolboy time too, though I would not have recognized the vintage. It may well have been a publicity shot from *The Man Who Fell to Earth*, in which, as the alien Thomas Jerome Newton, Bowie essentially played himself: soft-spoken and badly dislocated, politely paranoid, translucently beautiful. All director Nicolas Roeg had had to do was dress him more soberly; Bowie immediately adopted the look off-screen. Looking now at pictures of him in the mid 1970s, what strikes most people is just how crazily thin he was. It struck journalists at the time too, and there were even rumours about leukemia; or maybe the rumours, repeated in print, were meant to cover what everybody knew too well: that Bowie had found, as he later put it, a 'soulmate in cocaine'. But to an eleven-year-old he didn't look ill or addicted, just very strange indeed.

A man or a woman – impossible to tell! I had to find out more about David Bowie. Or rather that is how I've told the story for years: assuming that Bowie's image had snagged my imagination, that his androgyny already seemed a frail heroic affront to the world of the classroom, the playground, my devoutly strictured and emotionally hushed family. Can it be true? It's as likely I was merely amused: with his hat and his shades Bowie looked at best like a Hollywood starlet and at worst may have reminded me of well known cross-dressers of the time: TV comedians like Dick Emery. I might have been merely repelled, or shunned interest in case the familiar cry of 'Bender!' went up and my life was made a misery once more. But something of my interlocutor's enthusiasm surely took hold, and I now knew the name if little else.

11

This at least is certain: I spent the summer of 1981 listening to Bowie for the first time. National school was over, I had a black eye that lasted for weeks, and a friend had lent me a cassette of the compilation album *Changes One*, which once I'd got hold of my own copy was the only thing I owned by Bowie for the next two years. It was enough to be going on with: eleven songs, starting with 'Space Oddity', that I still cannot hear individually in other contexts (including their original albums) without predicting the next track from

Changes One or imagining it's time to flip the tape and start again after 'Golden Years'. I realized only later that the compilation – I'm not sure I even knew it *was* a compilation – covered a hectically varied span of Bowie's career up to the mid seventies; I don't recall noticing any transitions stylistically from space-age orchestral pop through aspirantly decadent rock to Bowie's 'plastic soul' phase. I do remember thinking that 'Space Oddity' was the best song, a work of mysterious genius that turned the sci-fi I was obsessed by into something altogether more elusive and spectral. Though I was reading Arthur C. Clarke around that time, and knew all about 2001 despite never having seen it, I had no sense that 'Space Oddity' was a 'novelty' record: it was just utterly beautiful and horribly sad, because after all a man was lost in space, and the circuit was dead, and how was he ever going to get home to his wife, whom he loved very much?

I would be retrojecting far too much in the way of self-discovery to say that by the time I arrived at secondary school in the autumn I understood much of what was going on in the other ten songs. The gay subtext – it is hardly a subtext – of 'John I'm Only Dancing' passed me by completely, though I guessed that the character (a louche amalgam of Jean Genet and Iggy Pop) to whom Bowie delivered the line 'let yourself go' in 'The Jean Genie' was not exactly being encouraged to give in to some conventional romantic boy–girl scenario. I knew in short that there was something weird about David Bowie, and 'weird' was exactly the word – a word with special currency among early-adolescent males – that was flung at me in the schoolyard when I announced excitedly that all summer I'd been listening to Bowie. Weird, and also queer. Somebody who must have known better than I did, a boy with an older sibling who was into Bowie, sneered when I mentioned the name: I'd been listening to a singer who had performed in a see-though jumper, maybe even a blouse. (The garment in question was at the V&A: one of the more sober Ziggy costumes.) I remember being embarrassed by the news that Bowie was a 'bender', and I think I kept quiet about him for a while, except to the friend who had lent me the tape in the first place, and to a cousin visiting from Canada, who was two years older and obsessed by the Who. I managed to persuade my parents to buy me a short book about Bowie from Eason's bookshop – little more than a discography with short accounts of each record's context – and it was in those pages that I discovered if not the full extent of the weirdness then at least its ambiguous outlines.

It is hard now to fully recover the cultural force that androgyny still possessed at the time I discovered Bowie. Never mind that his declared bisexuality – bruited to *Melody Maker* in 1972, lived down almost ever since – was largely decadent appliqué on legendarily prolific straight reality: I didn't know that at the time. What I had divined at the age of fourteen was that the songs I loved were frequently about gay desires or fantasized gay futures – I knew in short that there was a way of being and a culture that had nothing to do with playground taunts or camp acts on television. But Bowie's version of this, as expressed in his own persona, had more to do with some way of flamboyantly being-between, refusing the poles of gendered reality, than it did with the actuality of being gay; that was obvious even to a clueless teen. (There are people who have not forgiven Bowie for this, for his having it all ways with his adolescent audience in a period when many adults were agitating, in the wake of decriminalization in the UK, for a much greater acceptance of homosexuality than might be conjured by an arm around your guitarist on *Top of the Pops*.) In a way it is almost beside the point that I had myself, by my mid teens, fallen pathetically and silently in love with my best (male) friend at school, that I self-identified as bisexual till the point, some years later, that it became clear I really wasn't either. The larger lesson of Bowie's androgyny, and his avowed if equivocal bisexuality, a lesson I shared I suppose with many in my generation, was that sexual ambiguity was an ethic of sorts – a knight's move in the face of the fixed options of straight (and possibly also gay) identity.

12

Let us be clear: I was a Bowie fan and never a Bowie clone or, to use the term current in the 1970s, a casualty. You can see them in the old documentaries, and in the V&A's catalogue: tyro Ziggys of both sexes with their crudely feathered cuts and inexpertly applied glitter, preening outside concert venues. They had to move fast; a few months later they are sporting exaggerated 'gouster' suits and soul-boy dos, then before they know it fedoras and shades and tight little waistcoats: they sneer at the ones who still paint their faces with Aladdin Sane flashes, while Bowie speeds away from Victoria station in his open-topped car. I suspect that no pop star really attracted imitators in quite the same way before Bowie: yes, there had been quiffs and bowl cuts and skinny boys with fat lips and silk scarves, but none had so precisely, so desperately identified with their idol as to attain the status of clone. It is one of the things missing at the exhibition: there are several belated high-fashion retreads of key Bowie looks, but little sense of how far into the fabric of ordinary adolescent life his image had insinuated itself at the time. I arrived at Bowie far too late for all of that, though the back pages of music papers and shops in Dublin with names like Hairy Legs were still selling short powder-blue 'Bowie jackets' and prodigiously pleated 'Bowie trousers' in the mid 1980s. Who wore them? I never saw a Bowie casualty on the streets of Dublin. And when I say that he altered me forever as an adolescent, you would not have known it to look at me. The V&A insisted on the ways Bowie affected the texture and look of things, but somehow missed what he did to our insides.

13

The second time I cried at the V&A, I was standing in front of a screen that showed five minutes of Bowie's appearance on *Saturday Night Live* in December 1979. He's introduced by Martin Sheen: 'Ladies and gentlemen, David Bowie!' The camera pans to the singer and his band; at left on backing vocals are the performance artist Joey Arias and the mock-operatic New Wave German singer Klaus Nomi: a truly startling figure in tight black body stocking and chalk-white makeup. Bowie is stock still but for his flailing arms inside a gleaming black-and-white-striped funnel of sorts at centre stage: a costume based on Dadaist stage designs of the 1920s by Sonia Delaunay and Hugo Ball. (There are drawings and photos at the V&A, and the 1978 costume on a plinth.) Bowie sings 'The Man Who Sold the World': a song that is well known now thanks to Nirvana, but had then languished in relative obscurity, apart from a cover by Lulu in 1975, since he'd recorded it in 1970. I'd watched this clip at least a dozen times over the years. But still there was a moment, two verses in, just after Bowie delivered the line 'I smiled and shook his hand, and made my way back home'. Nomi and Arias come back with a half-synthesized 'Home!' It was that note that did it. I suppose it was the combination of such gleeful eclecticism and presence of mind with Bowie's frank nostalgia for his own song that set me off.

14

Everybody speaks of him as a cultural gateway – or is it gatekeeper? For many people, Bowie was, and maybe still is, the conduit towards an array of artistic and literary artefacts that the music, the image, the interviews make visible for the first time. The V&A has made much of the notion of Bowie as cultural switch or relay, though the exhibition stretches credibility in casting in terms of immersive influence his merely fashionable deployment of certain names: Nietzsche, Burroughs, Ballard and so on. This in the context of the late 1960s and early 1970s; later, it seems, Bowie did indeed become a manic autodidact on all kinds of topics. In any case, I can confidently list a good deal I would have either missed entirely or come to much later had it not been for Bowie: the musical stuff of course – Velvet Underground, Iggy, Roxy Music, T. Rex, Kraftwerk, Brian Eno – but also Warhol, Dalí (the books of both as much as the art), Brecht, Genet, Fassbinder, Nicolas Roeg. And yes: Nietzsche, Burroughs, Ballard. A predictable list, for sure; but it meant something to have been exposed to, or even just aware of, those figures aged thirteen instead of fifteen or sixteen, in part because it meant that the constellation of books and films and records that was revealed by those first few reference points was perhaps all the wider, and odder. Perhaps my favourite work of twentieth-century art is Andy Warhol's two-screen film portrait of Edie Sedgwick, *Outer and Inner Space*. I doubt Bowie ever saw it in the 1960s or 1970s, but there it was at the V&A, and who knows: I might never have got to it either had it not been for him.

Alongside the avant-garde and pop-cultural citations to follow up, there was the deeper lesson. It's customary to say that Bowie was the first postmodernist in pop music: that his borrowings from others, his inventions and reinventions of fantastical characters in the early 1970s, his control of his image to the extent that he could make a performance of exile and retreat in the second half of that decade, his ability to get away with being conventional because when he did it he did it with a wink – that all of this is in fact a study in effacing the distinction between surface and depth. It is true of course, and Bowie said as much very early on, announcing that rock music ought to embrace its whorish side. But it is not in the end quite so important as the other general good he preached. Bisexuality and androgyny were just the half of it: Bowie taught us, taught me, about the value of ambiguity. 'Is that a man or a woman, Dillon?' The question was as much about the image or the artefact as about the individual himself. A state of hovering, of ravishing indecision, seemed to define what art – music in the first instance, soon everything else – ought to be about, ought to deploy. Ambiguity became the ultimate artistic value for me, and I'm not sure that I have ever found a better, or even a more sophisticated, way of defining what I want from a song or a film or a poem or novel. For a time, as a teenager, when I had this word lodged in my head, I used to look at my father's bookshelves and the title of William Empson's *Seven Types of Ambiguity*, and think that I ought one day to read that book, but in the meantime the title was perfect.

15

His career in the 1980s was an education in cultural disappointment, a set of lessons in how artistic failure and commercial success might go hand in hand, and more importantly in the interior workings of that failure: the way an artist might lose it so comprehensively and remain convinced of his creative momentum, or at least of his legend. A lesson also in how to leave your heroes behind. All of that is familiar, and forgivable. Instead, here is a reminder of everything it was still possible to project on him at the height of his very mainstream return in 1983. A friend in the US emails me with her recollections of Bowie live at the Oakland Coliseum on September 17th that year, when she was fifteen. She keeps everything, and has just unearthed a note regarding her impressions of the concert. It's a mine of information: Bowie 'smiled a lot … wore hat later … undid bow tie … took off jacket, rolled up sleeves'. There was a call-and-response interlude during 'Fame', a bit of *Hamlet* business with cape and skull for 'Cracked Actor'. (The cape and the skull were at the V&A too.) The smile, she says, had obsessed her: the strange disparity between his big bland 1980s suits and the vampiric mouth full of European teeth. There are diary entries too, scribbled in front of the TV around midnight while waiting for him to appear: 'I have been so involved with Bowie all week … I HAVE TO CALM DOWN.'

16

Bowie at Live Aid, 13 July 1985. He has gathered a new band, accomplished but more than a little dull. He introduces them and gets a backing singer's name wrong, he fluffs a dance move and leaves his sax player stranded with her arm out towards him. He is wearing a light blue suit from the mid 1970s, the *Young Americans* period, specially tailored for the occasion. Chain-smoking on the helicopter on the way to Wembley, he boasts that the waist size is still the same. I know a lot of pointless facts about Bowie's appearance at Live Aid, but what I remember is this: that he wasn't very good. He seemed at once slick and stilted, the older songs not helped by airless mid-eighties perkiness. And I remember that I was hoping he would be good, really good, because a few miles away in hospital my mother was drifting in and out of consciousness and I was sure that she would die soon, and if David Bowie could only distract me for a few minutes and remind me why he still, just about, mattered to me, then things might be slightly more bearable.

17

On my way out of the V&A I bumped into a young journalist I'd met recently: she'd reviewed the exhibition and wondered what I thought. I shrugged and said I hadn't made up my mind, but then I brandished my bright orange Ziggy Stardust tote bag: it was David Bowie, after all, so how far wrong could the museum have gone? She sent me her review a few days later: 'It seems we disagree!' She had objected to what she called the 'morbidity' of the show, its treatment of Bowie as if he were already dead and canonized, his presence and his image constellated into a thousand relics. I couldn't disagree: how else to look at all those costumes in their vitrines, all those scraps of 1970s exercise books with their childish handwriting, the racks of vinyl

LPs to be flicked through like rosaries, the faces that are all one face looking down at us sternly or benignly, except with utter veneration? Morbidity was the point, fascination too. At its best, *David Bowie Is* turned its subject into a saint and a spectre. He must have known that it would.

18

David Bowie dead: imagine. I would guess that since my mid teens not a year has gone by without my daydreaming about the death of David Bowie. Some of these morbid interludes are easily explained: Bowie turns fifty and a glut of magazine and newspaper profiles ensues; Bowie speaks about the murder of his friend John Lennon; Bowie appears on an album cover, tending to the dead or dying body of his friend David Bowie; Bowie has a heart attack and effectively retires for the best part of a decade; Bowie turns sixty, heads towards seventy, gets photographed by the *Daily Mail* looking his age; some footage appears on TV of him chain-smoking Gitanes in the 1970s, or Marlboro Lights in the 1990s, and you wonder: how long can he carry on?

Or perhaps I think about the death of Bowie because in some involuted way that I have never described to anyone I have measured out my own life according to proximity or distance from his receding span. (Late 1980, Bowie appears fleetingly on an end-of-year pop awards show; I know who he is by now, but not how old – later I tell a cousin confidently: 'David Bowie is about fifty.') I almost never recall the dates of artists or writers I love; or rather, I remember when the likes of Beckett, Nabokov or Barthes died, but not when they were born. Warhol is an exception: born in 1928, like my father. And Bowie: 8 January 1947. I can always tell you how old he is; and so I always wonder, assuming the twenty-two years I have on him are any sort of advantage, what I'll be doing the day he dies: how I'll hear the news and what a fitting response might be. I'm ashamed to say that recently I have even wondered which YouTube clip I'd post to Facebook, in among all the links to 'Heroes' and 'Wild Is the Wind' and (God forbid) 'Ashes to Ashes'.

19

A rumour reaches me about Bowie: the sort of thing that has been all over the Internet for years, since his illness in 2004. The kind of rumour that you would think or hope his return might put to bed; but people seem to like this sort of conjecture, and here I am thinking about it despite myself. This time, the story arrives via friends who have friends who move in the kind of circles where people know such things, and where just as likely they invent those things, so as to make it seem as if their circle is fewer circles away from whatever coterie surrounds Bowie. So that while I hope the rumour is untrue, and I wish I had not heard it, I also don't believe it. But there it sits, an ugly piece of information, between me and the music, between me and all that Bowie has meant and not meant (all those records I ignored; perhaps I should have been paying attention?), in among the costumes and diary pages and video screens at the V&A.

20

The third time I cried I was standing with a good hundred others in one of the last rooms at the exhibition: a tall dimly lit space hung with huge screens on three sides, on which competing excerpts of concert footage from four decades were projected, and museum-goers stared upwards in the dark in a rather obvious approximation of the live experience, but not quite sure which Bowie they ought to be looking at. I thought, not for the first time, about the curious fate of '"Heroes"': a song that was hardly a hit in 1977, now widely thought his most sublime moment, but which rendered live has always been a shadow of the record. There have been very few cover versions of '"Heroes"': Blondie have performed it live since the 1970s; I have never heard, and hope I never will, the version recorded by *X-Factor* finalists in aid of injured British soldiers. In concert Bowie sounded as if he was singing a song not his own – as though it's been eroded out of his reach by overuse, like Leonard Cohen's 'Hallelujah'. I turned my back on '"Heroes"' and it died away in my ears. High in a far corner, fading up in the headphones now, was the Bowie of 1974: viciously thin and double-breasted, visored by those big sunglasses, hardly holding himself together. Once again it was the backing vocalists who got to me, buoying him up on the chorus: 'Boys, boys ... it's a sweet thing, sweet thing.'

Winnie

GWEN GOODKIN

It was the mid nineties and I was headed to the same town as her on a job laying foundation. I'd met Gizzard at the Rusty Nail just before I shoved off. He's the one told me where she was.

'Oxford. Ain't that just north of Cincinnati?' he'd said. 'You know Winnie Osterman's at the college there.'

Winnie had that rare mix of dark hair and blue eyes, and a body that curved just right. She was dangerous, too. Put herself in the hospital once. All of us boys wanted to get close to her, pass a palm over her flame, but she was Benji's girl. Now, word around town was they were through.

'I'll look her up,' I said.

'I bet you will.' He laughed, beer can held close to his mouth. 'Why don't you call her now?'

'You know same as me I don't have her number.'

'Ask her mom.'

I threw a five on the bar and let Royal know I was a goner. He gave me a nod. 'See you at Christmas, Gizz,' I said. 'Probably in this same stool.'

'If you're lucky,' he said.

I hauled my trailer down to Oxford and unhitched at the state park. Back then, Boss had me bouncing around the country to places like Knoxville and Bismarck, even down into Mexico, chasing whatever work a strip-mall developer threw at us. Campground life had become the norm. After a long string of nights by myself, I found the park's lone payphone and dialled.

'Winnie, it's RJ.'

She took a second. 'RJ?'

'Yeah,' I said. 'RJ Otto.'

'Holy shit,' she said. 'That took me by surprise.' She laughed and my mind went to her bare neck. 'How'd you get my number?'

'Your mom,' I said. 'I thought I could bring over some beer.'

'You're in Oxford right now?'

'Yeah,' I said. 'Here on a job.' I pulled a pack of matches from my pocket and lit one. I liked the smell.

'So you're bribing me with beer?' she said. 'Want me to help find you a college girl.'

'Something like that.'

'I like it,' she said. 'Tonight's out, though. I have an exam tomorrow. But –' She stopped to think. 'Maybe Wednesday.'

'Wednesday works,' I said. 'Tell me where you live and I'll be there at eight.'

I had two nights to think. Ironed my best shirt. Made sure my jeans were clean and my jaw was smooth. Last time I shaved at night must have been high school. I picked up a twelve-pack on the way and brought cigarettes just in case. Sometimes she smoked, sometimes she didn't.

What I expected of a college was noise – music and shouts and the whoop-whoop of kids on their parents' dime. This one was quiet. I held myself tight going up the dorm steps.

Next to her door a little sign said 'Jessica and Winifred'. No one back home, not even the teachers, called her Winifred. I'd assumed she was just plain Winnie. The door was open so I knocked on the metal frame. I poked my head around the corner. No one was there. Girls passed and gave me curious looks. I checked my watch. 7.59.

'RJ.' She walked toward me from the other end of the hall. Her long, dark hair flew with each step. *She must have a boyfriend* was all I could think. *If not, these college assholes are dumber than dirt.*

We hugged. She put her toothbrush away and pulled a jacket from her closet.

'Let's go,' she said.

'Where?'

'To a party.' She stopped. 'It's at a fraternity, so no outside guys. Don't worry, though, I'll sweet-talk them.' She motioned for me to give her the twelve pack. 'We can't get caught by campus police.' She opened the cardboard and stuffed some of the beers in her mini-fridge. She handed the box back to me bottom-heavy. 'You'll have to carry it under your coat.'

'I can drive,' I said.

'It'll be a hassle to find parking,' she said. 'Let's just walk.'

We talked about people from home. Who was getting married, which of those weddings were shotgun. Rumors of an affair between two teachers at school.

'Isn't it a pretty campus?' she said, looking up at the rooftops. All the buildings were light-red brick.

'Yeah,' I said. 'It's nice.' The beer was digging into my rib. 'Almost too perfect. Like it needs one of them oddball seventies spaceship buildings.'

She wrinkled her nose. 'No, I like that it's neat.' She stopped and pointed. 'See that small window high up?'

I tried to follow. 'No.'

She pulled me so close I knew what shampoo she used – the pink one that smelled like a Granny Smith. 'There. That's where I study.' We moved apart and started walking again. 'You're the only one who knows. I have to hide up there.'

I lifted a pack of cigarettes from the inside pocket of my coat. 'Why?'

'People think if they study with me, they'll get the same grades. They don't realize it doesn't work that way. Only I get the A.'

'But what does it hurt to study next to them?'

'Because they don't want me to study with them, they want me to study *for* them. I can't afford to help anyone. I'm here on scholarship.'

She asked me about work, and I told her how it'd taken me to Mexico a couple times. 'Some days it's hotter'n a bitch and you're working full sun and you curse the place. Can't get the smell of fried corn and diesel smoke off you. Old ladies selling warm cheese, flies all over and people buying. Beyond belief.' I pulled the plastic wrapper off the pack of cigarettes. 'But I'll tell you what. I'm the first to raise my hand whenever a job down there comes up.'

'Why?'

I saw a bench and set the beer down. 'Soon as you cross the border, the tightness leaves your shoulders. Well – after you pass the guy with the machine gun.' I fished some matches out of my coat. 'The food's good. Real cheap, too. And, the women are nice.' I shook out a cigarette.

'In bed?'

I lit the cigarette. 'Hell no,' I said. 'Don't want 'em nice in bed.'

Neither of us would look away. She smiled first, though.

'Want it?' I asked, holding the cigarette toward her.

'Like, yesterday,' she said.

I lit another.

'Think you'll ever leave town for good?'

I shook my head. 'All my friends are there.'

'Guys are funny. They make friends in first grade and those are all the friends they need. Girls have about twelve different best friends in life.'

We headed down a side street.

'Think you'll move back home?' I asked. We were at the bottom of the fraternity's porch steps. 'Or leave for good?'

She dropped her cigarette and stepped on it. 'I'm already gone, baby.'

A guy leaned against the doorframe with his arms crossed. He wore big, loose jeans and a baseball cap. I couldn't see his eyes, he wore the hat so low. And there was a hoop earring through the brim. He'd actually thought that out.

'Hi, Jason,' said Winnie. She gave him a big, slow hug and he pulled her close to his waist, all the while staring in my direction.

'Where's everybody else?' he asked.

'They'll be here soon,' she said.

'Who's this?'

'This is RJ,' she said. 'He's my cousin. He's just here for a visit.'

'Your cousin.'

'Yeah,' she said. 'And look – we brought beer.'

I pulled the box from my coat and offered it to him. He looked inside and pulled out three beers – he kept two for himself and gave one to Winnie.

'Come in,' he said. 'It's a ghost town right now. That'll change in an hour.'

He moved over just enough for us to pass, then caught Winnie by the wrist. 'I'll see you later,' he said.

She flicked the brim of his hat. 'Promise?' He had to take it off to set it back straight. He had small eyes set close together. Smart to keep them covered.

We walked toward what looked like a home library, all dark wood, fat armchairs and navy carpet. 'That guy at the door,' she whispered. 'His dad is the president of Ace Hardware or some shit.' She took a gulp of beer. 'He's loaded.'

I looked around at the library with its dusty books and paisley wallpaper and wondered what the hell I was doing there.

'Most of the kids here are.'

'Are what?'

'Loaded.' She took another drink. 'One of the girls I hang out with is from New York City and has a driver. Another has her own sailboat. I don't mean her family has a sailboat, I mean her family has a sailboat *and* she has her own sailboat.' She finished her beer and waved at me for another.

I could tell she liked it in a way, being around all these people. Maybe she thought their money was going to rub off on her. I took out the last two beers and flattened the cardboard. A couple girls passed the doorway, saw us and kept walking. I lit two cigarettes. 'You ever talk to Benji?'

She pressed her lips together. 'Never.'

'You want to?'

'Nope,' she said. 'Over and done.'

I ashed in my empty. 'Got a boyfriend?'

She stared at the carpet. 'No boyfriend.'

'Why?'

'I was with one person all of high school,' she said. 'Not doing that again.'

The door from the basement opened and the music flared then the door shut and it was only bass again. 'Don't tell me you're sleeping around?'

'I wouldn't call it sleeping.'

That got me mad. 'Don't do that to yourself.'

She turned cold. 'You do it.'

'Where you get that?'

We faced each other. She moved close enough to me to where I could smell the apple again. 'Mexico.'

Someone shouted 'Hey!' in an angry voice that made us flinch. Jason came toward us in big strides. 'No smoking in the library.'

Winnie and I looked at our cigarettes as if we'd never seen them before.

'Sorry, man.' I dropped mine in the can. Winnie pushed hers in after.

He studied her, then me. 'Intense conversation for a pair of cousins.'

'We aren't cousins,' I said.

'Oh, really,' he said. 'You're a tricky one, Winn.' He turned to me. 'How do you know Winn then?'

I laughed through my nose. Who was this guy? 'Winnie and I go way back. Clear to kindergarten, ain't it?'

She nodded. The door opened and there was the music again, full volume.

'Are you going downstairs?' Jason pressed Winnie to his side and she hugged his waist and he picked her up like he was carrying her over the threshold and started toward the basement. She pretended to be annoyed, but I could see she loved it.

'Come on, RJ,' she called over his shoulder.

'I think I'll head out.' I wedged my empty into the corner of an armchair.

She told Jason to wait and he put her down. She came over to me. 'You're leaving? We just got here. You haven't even met my friends.'

'I gotta be up early.'

'You should stay,' she said. 'I've got some cute friends …' She raised her eyebrows.

'Thanks,' I said. 'But I'll leave you to your party.' I gave her a tight hug and whispered in her ear. She covered a smile with her hand.

'Careful,' I'd said. 'Them big jeans are for hiding small dicks.'

I didn't call her again. And after a month I damn near forgot about her. Then I heard a knock on the trailer door. I checked the TV to make sure it wasn't the show, then answered.

'Winnie Osterman,' I said. 'I'll be goddamned.' There she stood, her hair shining in the moonlight, hands in her jacket pockets. 'How'd you find me?' I waved her inside. She stepped up and looked around.

'Your truck was parked out front.'

'But it's a new truck,' I said.

'County's on the plate.'

I turned down the TV and handed her a beer. She sat next to me on the bench around the table. Only place to sit really. We drank a bit. She took the cigarette I offered.

'You know what I'm going to ask.'

She picked a piece of tobacco from her tongue. 'I'm homesick is all.'

'Next time call me,' I said. 'I'll pick you up. I don't like you driving out here by yourself.'

'I didn't drive here,' she said. 'My friend brought me.' She pushed off her shoes. 'She told me I was crazy and didn't want to leave me here, but I made her go when I saw your light on.'

So she planned to stay. We traded bits of gossip about people from home. Friends breaking up. Car accidents. People who'd quit school to work out at the plant. Then she said, 'RJ, why'd you call me?'

I shrugged, 'Homesick is all.'

We both smiled.

'Anyone ever tell you how pretty you are?'

She plucked the tab on her beer can. 'Once or twice.'

I kissed her, slow at first, then we couldn't get rid of our clothes fast enough.

'I have bad news.' I pointed at the bed. 'The sheets are outside drying.'

She laughed and I went outside pecker swinging. I didn't care. No one to see me anyway. I put them sheets on in record time. She was on top of me and I couldn't stop touching her skin. 'Winnie,' I said into her hair. 'Winnie.'

'I got milk and cereal,' I said when she woke up. 'But I buy my coffee at the gas station.'

'Gas station coffee is fine with me,' she said.

'Come on, get dressed.'

She propped herself up on an elbow. 'You can't go alone?'

'I can,' I said. 'But I don't want to.'

And then we kissed and I ran my fingertips clear down to the bottom of her spine and past it, to the back of her soft thighs until she shivered on top of me.

'I mean it this time,' I said. 'I got to get to a phone.'

'Why?'

'To call in to work.' I lit a cigarette and pulled on my jeans.

'I have to go back,' she said. 'I have class.'

'You can skip it once, right?'

She pulled her hair into a ponytail, said nothing.

'Let's get a real breakfast.' I said. 'Eggs and bacon.'

After we ate, she wanted to go back to the dorm to shower and brush her teeth.

'You can shower at my place,' I said.

'But I need to brush my teeth,' she said. 'And change my clothes.'

'I'll stop and get you a toothbrush.' I pulled into the gas station. 'And you look real good in the clothes you're wearing.'

'I need clean underwear.'

'Skip the underwear.'

She pulled out her ponytail and redid it. 'You just don't want me to go back to school.'

'Correct.'

'Why?'

'Who'd let a pretty girl like you out of his sight?' I offered her my hand. She stared at it. 'Come on, now.' She took my hand and scooted across the bench seat.

When I stepped out of the shower, she was combing her wet hair with her fingers and still wrapped in a towel. That came off real quick.

She was on my lone pillow. I'd bunched up a sweatshirt for myself. Our legs were together. She rubbed the calluses at the base of my fingers.

'What's it like?' she said. 'Your job.'

'Sometimes at the end of the day, my hands feel like they're casted in cement. All the dust on them hardens and I want them to move, but it's like they're molded in place,' I said. 'First thing tomorrow and clear till the end of the day I'll catch hell for missing work. We're already behind schedule and the customer's laying into us for starting late on account of all the water we hit when we dug the footings. Now we got to put antifreeze in the cement because we're up against winter. This is all boring to you.'

She turned my hand over and studied it. 'I like to hear you talk,' she said. 'Makes me feel like I'm sitting in front of a fire.' She ran a finger across my palm.

I flinched. 'Tickles.'

She did it again. I held my hand steady and stared at her.

'What's the J in your name stand for?' she asked. 'James?'

I felt the stubble above my lip. I needed to shave. 'J is for Junior. Though my pop wishes he'da saved that for my brother.'

'Oh, you can't mean that,' she said and kissed a callus.

'Sure as shit I do,' I said. 'He tells me every chance he gets.'

She stretched the sheet tight over her legs and tucked it deep under her thighs. 'Dads,' she said. 'Can't live with 'em, can't live without 'em.'

'I don't know what you're talking about,' I said. 'From what I can tell, you won the dad lottery.' I pushed my fingers between hers. 'When I think about your dad, I picture him mowing the lawn in his German hat, smoking his pipe. He seems like a pretty happy-go-lucky guy.'

She pulled her fingers free of mine. 'He sure has you fooled.'

I didn't know what to do – leave it at that or ask her to explain. Now I wish I'd stood up, got dressed and convinced her to walk the campground with me. Changed the scenery.

She jumped out of bed and started putting her clothes on. 'Everyone in town thinks he's such a nice guy,' she said. 'And they'll never think anything different because they don't want to. That's how it is.'

I walked to the fridge and poured her a glass of milk. She drank some. Neither of us spoke. I pulled on some shorts, turned on the TV and let her come to me. She did eventually and things between us were more careful, like we were setting the table with the good dishes.

'So, then – what is your middle name?' She took a sip of milk.

'Christopher,' I said.

'RC,' she said. 'Like the drink.'

'Yep.'

'That'll be my nickname for you,' she said. 'Cola.'

I turned one of her wrists over, ran my thumb across the soft side and felt two vertical scars. I stared at them.

'If you cut the length of each vein, you bleed more,' she said.

'How did you even know to do that?'

She finished the last of her milk. 'You can find anything out if you want to.'

When I woke in the morning, she was gone. I found a note in the kitchen that said, 'Goodbye, Cola.' I threw on my jeans and jumped in the truck. She couldn't have walked. It was too far. I drove slow and searched the side of the road. I parked in the first space I saw at the dorm and thought for a while about what to do. I went to the front door and waited for someone to come out. Last time, I'd only stood there a few seconds. This time it seemed like minutes. I nodded a thank you and took the steps two at a time. When I reached her door I went to knock and heard her voice inside. I stood there, unsure of what to do. Then I took a step back, then another and I turned around and headed for the stairs.

I found Gizzard just where I left him. 'Tell me you've been home once or twice since I saw you last,' I said. We slapped each other's shoulders and I settled into my stool. We shot the shit for a while and then he asked: 'Did you call?'

I lit my cigarette. 'Bet your ass I did.'

He was surprised. 'And?'

'And I brought her some beer.'

'That's it?'

'Mostly,' I said.

'What do you mean, "mostly?"' He raised his eyebrows.

If I told him, he'd expect an explanation – what happened, what I'd done wrong. I didn't want to get into it. I said nothing.

'You're a chump then,' he said. 'How do you blow a chance like that?'

I lifted off my seat to get a view of the back. 'Have you seen her?'

'Nope.' He raised his empty at Royal. 'You,' he said, pushing his middle finger between my top ribs, 'fucked up.'

Just after the new year I was hitching my trailer to my truck out back at Mom and Dad's. It was so cold I had to talk myself into touching the metal winch.

'RJ.'

That made me jump. I banged my knee against the winch and yelped in pain. There she stood, covering a laugh.

'That ain't funny.'

'I'm sorry,' she said, still laughing.

I rubbed my knee then shook it out. 'I'm going to start calling you The Magician. Never know where you'll appear,' I said. 'Or disappear.'

She stared at the frozen mud then eventually met my eyes. 'Can I explain?'

'You don't need to,' I said. 'Want to go inside?'

She shook her head and jammed her hands in her coat pockets. 'You don't know what it's like down there. All those rich kids. I do what I can to fit, but I'm not one of them. And it seems like …' She lifted her face toward the grey clouds. 'The harder I try, the plainer it gets: I'm somewhere I don't belong.'

My fingers were going numb. 'Then stop trying.'

She sighed. We were facing each other now. 'It's my only way out.'

I pointed a thumb at the trailer. 'I'm almost ready to go.' The snow had started, a flake or two at a time. 'You could come with me. Leave the snow for the sunshine. And peaches. Lots of them in Georgia.'

She backed away. 'I can't.'

'Just drive down with me. If you don't like it, I'll take you back to school.'

'No,' she said. 'I can't.'

After the Georgia job I jumped at a gig down in Chihuahua. I met Lorena there and decided to stay. Found work with an American putting up apartment buildings.

A few years later I brought Lorena home with me for Christmas. We went to the Rusty Nail and I opened the door expecting to see Gizzard front and centre, but his seat was empty. I searched the bar and spotted him at the pool table. We went up to him and I gave him a slap on the back.

'Hey Gizz,' I said. 'Meet my girl.' I had my arm around Lorena's shoulders, proud of how pretty she was. Her and Gizzard shook hands. Then he said, 'Lorena, this is my wife Winnie.'

I hadn't recognized her. She'd puffed up, cut off her hair and put some skunk-looking stripes in it.

'Winnie Osterman?' I said, still not believing. 'What happened to your hair?'

She laughed. 'I take it you don't like it.'

'You guys are married? When'd that happen?'

'Two months ago,' said Gizzard. He pulled her close.

She shook her can and finished the last drink. 'I came to the bar a few years back, couple days after New Year's. I'd gone to your parents' and your mom said you'd just left but you might have stopped here on your way out.' She looked at me, then away. 'And there was Gizzard.'

I clapped Gizz on the shoulder. 'Well, bud,' I said. 'I wouldn't've put money on it, but ...' I needed a second before I could get it out. 'Congratulations.'

'You, too, Cola,' Winnie said and nodded at Lorena, who was talking to Benji's latest model-type girlfriend.

Benji was coming toward us, behind Winnie and Gizz. He tilted his head at Winnie and wiped fake sweat off his forehead, mouthing 'whew'. *Dodged that bullet.*

'Cola?' said Gizzard.

'Old joke,' I said, embarrassed for her – reaching for something that wasn't there. I changed the subject. 'Where you putting that fancy degree to use?'

'Oh, no degree,' she said. 'I dropped out.' Gizzard kept her close enough that she had to lean my way to be heard. 'I'm a teller at the bank.'

'Teller's a good job,' I said. 'But why quit school?'

She finished her beer and handed her empty to Gizz. 'Got to be too much,' she said. 'All the back and forth.'

Gizz left to get another round.

'I never told him about us,' I said to her.

'I know,' she said.

'I never told him nothing.'

That was fifteen years ago. Soon after, the plant shut its doors and left for Mexico. People wanted their TVs big as couches and dirt cheap and they couldn't have both with American labour. The Rusty Nail closed down. A trinket shop took its place, selling greeting cards and teddy bears.

I don't get back to town much. We've been in Dallas eight years, raising our two girls. I own a construction company, which keeps me moving at an ungodly pace. From what I hear, Winnie and Gizzard had a couple kids of their own. Gizzard started driving truck when the plant pulled out. Whenever Mom gets me on the phone, which isn't often I'm ashamed to say, she tells me the town gossip.

'That classmate of yours, the Osterman girl – what's her name?'

'Winnie.' I'm in the garage, squeezing wood glue on a split picture frame.

'Yeah, well. She made manager at the bank,' says Mom. 'Hold on a second. Let me get my coffee.'

That time with all of us at the bar at Christmas, when Winnie and me talked, a country song came on.

'I love this song,' she said to me.

'You know this is "Cadillac Ranch",' I said. 'Springsteen wrote it.'

'Springsteen sucks,' she said, then kept singing, 'Cadillac, Cadillac. Long and dark, shiny and black.'

'Sounds like he's singing about the unit he wishes he had,' I said. We cracked up and there it was, the moment she'd been reaching for.

Mom's back on the phone. 'Where was I?'

'Winnie.'

'Now that she's a big shot, they had to run out and buy Louie Croy's house.' Mom blows on her coffee and takes a sip. 'Poor old Croy wasn't even cold in the grave before that son of his had the house for sale.'

I grab an old cloth to clean up the glue drips. 'Sounds about right,' I say.

'You know what house I'm talking about.'

'Sure,' I say, though I can't recall it.

'Wonder what Greg thinks.' She refuses to call him Gizzard.

My daughter opens the door from the kitchen and waves me inside for dinner. 'What he thinks about what?'

'Why,' says Mom, 'about living right aside her parents.'

At the Rusty Nail, when the song's chorus started up again in the bar, Winnie sang, 'Cadillac, Cadillac. Long and dark –' She held her hands about a foot apart and sang her own version in my ear: 'Big black unit.'

I forced a smile. The moment was over.

'It's really about a hearse,' I said. I don't know if she heard me, though.

Care kids

COLIN MURPHY

Three years ago, I wrote a long piece for this magazine about a woman named Linda Lambe, who died in 2007. In a life marked by an intellectual disability and chronic homelessness, Linda had had nine children, all of whom were taken into state care. One of her children was a boy named Danny Talbot, who died in 2009; the circumstances of his death were documented, anonymously, alongside those of 195 other children and young adults who had been in care (or were 'known to the child protection services'), in the Report of the Independent Child Death Review Group, published last year. This work opened a window for me onto a world I hadn't known existed. This was the world of the care system.

There are now roughly six thousand children in state care, which means that legal responsibility for their welfare resides with the Health Service Executive (HSE) rather than their parents. The vast majority of these children are in foster homes. Some four hundred children are in what is known as 'residential care', living in centres run by the HSE or by private contractors. Sometimes this is because the child didn't adapt well to initial foster placements, or because he or she came into care late and the HSE was unable to find an appropriate foster home; other times it is because the child displayed behavioural or other problems that required specialized care and therapeutic services, or, in rare cases, secure detention.

In Dublin there are also hostels for homeless teenagers, which are used by the HSE's 'crisis intervention service' to house young people who need emergency accommodation. This service is known, colloquially, as the 'out of hours' because it is available outside of working hours. To access it, the young person reports to a Garda station at night, from where a duty social worker is called and a hostel placement is arranged, if possible.

When a young person in care turns eighteen, he or she is discharged from the care of the state and allocated an 'aftercare' worker to help them with their dealings with state agencies and to offer guidance and support. The aftercare worker may help the young person find supported accommodation with a private aftercare provider and may arrange funding from the HSE for various needs. Typically, this service continues until the age of twenty-one; if the young person is in full-time education, aftercare may be extended.

There is, however, no legal right to aftercare, and its provision is extremely patchy. Young people and care workers I have spoken to say that the support offered is often inadequate and that its quality varies hugely according to location. They say it is anomalous that those in full-time education, whose circumstances are apparently most secure, have greater access to aftercare than those who may be more vulnerable.

The stories that follow are those of four young people, now aged between nineteen and twenty-three, who have been in the care of the HSE. I met them through two organizations: the After Residential Care Trust, based in Co. Kildare, and EPIC (which stands for 'empowering people in care'), based in Smithfield, Dublin. I met other young people who were generous and courageous in sharing stories which, for various reasons, I have not included here. The accounts below are based on recorded interviews. I transcribed the interviews, edited the transcripts and gave them to the subjects for approval. I did not include information or opinion that reflected on other identifiable individuals, except a minimal amount of information on their parents, where this was relevant to establishing why they had been taken into state care. References to the names of specific institutions have also been omitted in cases where descriptions of conditions in those institutions could have been seen to reflect on staff. But the accounts by these four young men and women do include information and opinion relating to their interaction with the HSE. Although much of this would be impossible to verify (the HSE, correctly, will not comment on individual cases), it seemed to me that to strip these accounts of any direct or implied criticism of the HSE would undermine their integrity and do a disservice to the young people concerned. These are their stories; for large periods of their lives, the HSE took responsibility for their care; if they feel that care was inadequate, they are entitled to say so. These criticisms are echoed in numerous other accounts I have been given by people associated with the system and young people who have been in care.

The HSE, of course, is the Irish public health system, funded by the Irish state and overseen by the Department of Health. To the extent that the HSE took the place of these young people's parents, it did so on behalf of the state and, therefore, of the public. Its failings are our failings.

My research for this article has been supported by the Mary Raftery Journalism Fund.

Sarah

I went into care when I was two. They found a dead body in my house. She was only about eighteen. My parents were drug addicts: she had overdosed with them and that's how she died. They had to take all us children out, and we all got split up. I was put with a series of foster families. But I didn't get along with them and didn't like getting moved from family to family. I just wanted my own, I guess. I ended up going from foster family to residential placement to foster family to residential placement to on the streets to off the streets – back and forth, really. I was in about twenty-five placements altogether.

I first went into residential care when I was about seven, into a home in Dublin. I remember exactly what my social worker told me: 'You don't have to go to foster placements any more – no new families for you.' I seen this big playground in between these two big houses and I just thought, 'This is the life. This is going to be great craic.' And by God, was it a smack of reality that night. I'm a real fussy eater and I didn't eat the food. I remember them telling me: 'That's not how it works here, honey. You eat what's cooked for you in this house. You eat what's given or you don't eat at all.'

I remember kids outside the gate and their ma's saying to them, 'If you're bold, that's where you're going.' And we'd be sitting inside the gate and it's like they see you as invisible. And you're like, 'I'm *here*! Just because I don't have parents doesn't mean that doesn't hurt.' You'd always hear, 'Orphan Annie, Orphan Annie, Orphan Annie'. I got awful bullied in primary school 'cause all the kids in the estate knew what the home was. They just used to eat into us: 'There's them care kids, there's them care kids.' That's all you'd hear. I think the name just stuck with all the care kids. Now it's the name that care kids have for themselves.

It's very hard to try to keep control of your life when you're in care 'cause you have one set of friends that are from one part and you've another set of friends from another part, so you've friends all over; it's very hard to grasp real friends and hold onto them. Where junkies would have their junkie friends and alcos have their alco friends, care kids tend to have their care kid friends, 'cause their lives are chaotic as well. Because when you're going out with normal friends that have mams and dads, they have no clue, they have no idea, and it's so hard to even try and explain your life to them.

It's hard living in a residential. You have twenty or thirty staff coming in daily, telling you what you can and can't do, telling you that you can't phone your family. Loads of times, I'd try and run out the gate and they'd grab me and pull me into the house and lock me into this room called the 'cushion room'. Care kids would know what it is. It's a solitary room where there's just the four box walls and cushions and they just fuck you in there and if you run amuck in there they'll just go in there and restrain you: it's their way of pulling you away from the rest of the house so it doesn't act up. You could be sitting in there all night. I remember having to break windows because I couldn't breathe – if you're claustrophobic and you're in a boxed room and there's somebody sitting on you, restraining you, by the time they get off you, you're, like, you can't breathe, and so you're trying to get out a window, and so you smash a window. So when it's written in a report about care kids that they smashed a window, that they did this and that, it makes it look really bad: makes you look like you're mad, going around putting out windows, breaking up the place; but people don't realize that there's a story behind every action.

Care kids are very good at listening and observing. They understand a lot quicker than an average kid would. They want to know what adults are saying. When you see two adults talking you always think: 'They're talking about me, they're giving out about me ... Why are they talking about me? ... I have to have done something ... What have I done? ... They're talking ... They're giving out ... It's a *meeting*.' Because everything is a meeting.

I was in that residential for about five years. It ended up falling apart 'cause I just think I'd had enough. I'd had enough of the HSE. I ended up breaking up the house one night and left. I went into town and stayed in my friend's for a few days. If I hadn't had her, where else would I have went? I don't have any family. That's what people don't understand: most people have aunts, uncles to fall back on. The HSE rely on them to pick up the pieces. I was in care all my life. Where was I going to go? I was trying to avoid going to the homeless service. My sister and a lot of my friends were in it: I didn't want to go through them doors, because I knew it was harsh.

I called the social worker. People think your social worker is your guardian angel; the truth is the complete opposite. It's like nine to five: if you ring after five, you're definitely not getting through; if you ring before five, you might get a voicemail. It was hard enough to keep track of your social worker, because one year you could have a social worker and by next week you could have a different one, there was just so many of them, and you wouldn't even know that you had a different one. 'Go to the Garda station,' she said. I went to the station: the guard said, 'Listen, love, I can't ring the out-of-hours before six o'clock. Come back in two hours.' I was with a friend; the two of us sat in McDonald's, in the toilets, and just cried our hearts out. That first night, I got a bed in Lefroy House [a *Salvation Army hostel in Dublin providing emergency beds for young people*]. I was the youngest in Lefroy; my sister had been in there two nights previously. It has four or five bedrooms; you have your lockers and your kitchen with a camera watching you. But if your stuff goes missing, it's your problem. They'll make you a toastie, or sometimes you're in time for dinner. You've to be out by nine in the morning. During the day, you literally just walk around town and hope to God that your social worker is going to ring, or that something is going to help you. You're just sitting in McDonald's, without paying for anything, trying to charge your phone, hoping they won't kick you out 'cause you haven't bought anything. Thank God, I had friends around town.

You see a lot of things in hostels, things you shouldn't see. I remember seeing people gearing up in hostels. My first night in the hostels, the next morning I got a syringe put up to me outside the door to take me phone off me. If the beds in the hostels are all filled, tough titty, you're sleeping on the floor of Store Street or Kevin Street [Garda stations]; if you're lucky, the guards might let you into a cell. Supposedly it's meant to be an emergency service but I spent months in and out of the 'out-of-hours' service. It's a real eye-opener: you really are on your own and it makes you see things from a different angle. You're walking in the street past all these people that are meant to be 'society' and you're, like, left walking around hungry, cold, and none of them could give a flying fuck.

I was a few months in the out-of-hours service. Then I went to a private placement for a month. Then I went to another private placement for a month. I ended up going to me sister's house and staying there, till they got another placement for me. Then, when me sister died, that's when it all spiralled out of control again. [Sarah's sister died of a drug overdose.] I just thought everyone was to blame for me sister dying: loads of people could have prevented it but they didn't. My sister was eighteen when she died; she grew up in care, like me, and she had a horrendous life, much worse than me. She never settled, till the day she died.

I didn't want to go homeless and I didn't want to end up going down the road that my sister went. So I took an overdose. I remember them saying in the hospital, 'You're so lucky to wake up,' and I said to the doctor, 'I don't want to wake up, I don't want to be alive. Who wants to be in the world when it's like this?' I was like, nobody cared about my sister when she died and nobody's going to give a fuck about me when I die. I was like, let me be another number for their records, I don't care. I just had had enough of it.

[*Sarah recovered and, after a number of further placements, went to live with Sharon and her family; Sharon had previously been a care worker in a centre in which Sarah had been placed.*] I get to see my sisters and brothers once a month. That's put together by the HSE. It's called 'sibling access'. They get your family and they have a social worker sitting there and they supervise it and we all get a visit for an hour and a half. It used to be in Superdome leisure centre or bowling alleys, not even in a visiting centre or anything like that. That's not the right place to have a visit if you want to ask your family questions. The HSE have rules around access: you can't go into the past too much; they say there's another place and time for that. They tell you that you can't tell your siblings certain stuff about your family, like about my sister dying; they'd say, 'Don't be saying things like that around your little sister.' But they should know that they have a big sister that died. Why should you block that off from them? I feel like the HSE just pull families apart.

That's the one thing about being a care kid: there is no line of trust. You can't trust nobody when you're in care. You stick to yourself. A lot of kids when they're new in care think it's great; they think everyone that smiles at them is their friend. And it's not that way at all because the person that's smiling straight to your face and asking you loads of questions is the first person that's talking behind your back. You can't trust no one. Even the friend that you're hanging out with, you can't trust them 'cause your stuff goes missing.

I have got a bond with Sharon and I do trust a little. But I wouldn't trust a lot. You can't trust anyone fully. Because anyone can switch. People change their minds like the weather. With a care kid, it kind of sticks to you more. You nearly reject them before they reject you. You're like, 'I'm going! I'm packing my stuff! I'm leaving, I'm not staying here!' Care kids tend to be like that: they'll reject you before you reject them or if they think for one minute that you're thinking of it.

I am a system child. This is what happens when the system rears you.

Alan

I was put into to care when I was nine years of age. There was lot of trouble going on in the family, and other stuff I don't want to talk about. I had about thirteen care placements in all. I couldn't handle it at the foster homes: waking up every morning, coming down and seeing them as a family and then seeing myself as an outsider. So I'd just take myself back upstairs.

Then I went into residential care. It was better; I wasn't waking up and seeing the same people every day. There was two staff members each day and they'd come in and help you with everything you needed; if you wanted help with your cooking or cleaning, they'd help you out.

I got into a good bit of trouble and ended up getting locked up in Oberstown for three weeks. It's a place for – as they like to call it – 'young offenders'. When I got there, it changed in my head. People look at me, they see my baggy clothes and Adidas and McKenzie and my tattoos, and they think I'm a scumbag. But in there, you see all these scumbags, with scars on their faces, and I was thinking, I don't want to be like them. It kind of changed my life. I seen two pathways: one path was a life of crime and the other path was just stay out of it. I kind of started again in life and stayed out of trouble. Like, there has been a few incidents where I did get in trouble, but nothing serious happened over it.

When I was eighteen, I got put into an apartment of my own. Some people will think it's great to have an apartment at the age of eighteen but it's actually not all fun and games. It was kind of lonely and depressing, not having anyone there. There was bills – I just couldn't handle them. There was no one really there to support to me. I'd have my shower and then basically just sit on the couch, really. Smoke fags. Just sit there all day and just think, think, think, think. And then at night just go back to bed, and start it all over again next morning. Me head just got a bit melted.

I fell into a state of depression, just wondering, like, 'When I am going to get kicked out?' And then after six months I got kicked out, put out onto the street. I rang the After Residential Care Trust and they sent me to a homeless shelter where I am currently staying. I'm sharing a room with a fifty-two-year-old man. We're put out every morning at nine o'clock and have to wait till half five to get back in.

Sometimes, you know, I do have a bit of anger in me. Just thinking back over all the days when I wasn't with me family. Thinking where my life has gone. That gets me a bit upset. And when I dance, it just relieves all the stress. It gets me away. It's the only thing that I really like to do. It's the main talent that I have.

I've been dancing for about three years now. The movie *Step Up* – that inspired me. So I taught myself for a year and then ended up going to dance classes and it just picked up from there. I do hip-hop and breakdancing. The hip-hop is more a dance of anger: there's a lot of moves in there that will be difficult; you'll put your mind to it and it will get you off the anger and everything.

I'm teaching my own classes now. I'd like to go further. I want to do choreography for famous people, be in dance videos, dance movies; anything that involves dance, I'll do it. The main point is to work hard, stay at it, pick up more moves on the way up. I rehearse in my room in the hostel, every night.

Danielle

I was taken into care when I was fifteen and at first I was placed in emergency accommodation. I didn't like it at all, 'cause I would have got beaten a lot by older kids. I wouldn't have been streetwise at all, being placed from the country smack in the city centre of Dublin. But that taught me a lot for when I moved out into the residential centre: like, not to hand anyone my phone, 'cause they'd rob my phone on me.

Before I went into care I would have been suicidal and self-harming a lot, cutting my wrists, wanting to take my own life. And then when I went into care, it got worse, 'cause I started talking about a lot of things. It really, really got hard for me. I was using a lot of drugs to try and cope with my mental health.

I literally just hit rock bottom. I tried to hang myself. I was put on twenty-four-hour watch. Every five minutes, someone was coming in and checking on me. I was in and out of A&E. But I don't like sitting and waiting; I get really agitated in groups of people. So I ran off [back to the residential centre].

I remember lying on my couch in the house, seeing flashing lights. I got up and looked out the window. There was an ambulance. I turned around. There were four staff members, the house manager, the team leader of the social work department, two medics and two guards. And they were bringing me in the back of the ambulance to St James's. I was like, What is going on? The first thing I asked was, 'Can I go and get a bag of clothes?' They were like, 'No'. No one told me anything about this. They went and got a court order for me to be placed in hospital. [*Under the Mental Health Act 2001, the HSE can apply to the District Court for the involuntary admission of a child to a psychiatric facility.*]

I got out of the ambulance outside the main entrance of the hospital and walked up to the ward. The ward was basically just one massive, long corridor and I went to leg it and the two guards just latched on to me. I was bawling my heart out. I wouldn't talk to anyone. I hated everybody for putting me in there. I just wanted to be out. The first week, all I done was cry. I remember one patient to a tee. She was walking really, really slow, highly medicated, and when you walked by her, she'd try to grab you. She'd just scare the bleeding daylights out of you, properly. My nephew came in to see me, and one of the patients barged into my room and tried to grab my nephew. I grabbed her and threw her up against a pillar. I remember people being sedated on the corridor. And people walking around like zombies cause they're that highly medicated. There was nothing for me to do.

I don't believe in taking medication. I believe in reiki and acupuncture and all that, 'cause it's better for you in the long run. I was sixteen, the youngest person in that ward. The closest person to my age would have been twenty-odd. It's not appropriate for a sixteen-year-old child to be in an adult mental health hospital. There's nowhere out there for kids of that age, from sixteen to eighteen. There's nothing. The only reason I was placed in the hospital was 'cause they couldn't get a bed to suit me anywhere else. I wasn't diagnosed with any mental health illness. I just needed the security and somewhere safe, and to actually be able to sit down and talk to people and work out my problems and how to cope when I get stressed. When I was in special care, later, I done all of that. Because I had no choice. I was in a confined place. I wasn't allowed out 24/7; I had no phone. ['Special care' units provide more intensive and specialized support for young people than normal residential centres. They are locked units: the young person is legally detained there under court order.]

I was in the special care unit when I found out about family history. I robbed my file out of the office. I would never usually do something like that. I was just really frustrated and I went down and locked myself into the TV room. All the staff were trying to get in. I was like, What's in this file? I handed the file back to the staff then, after I read it. Then, two days later, my social worker came in and met with me and told me exactly what had happened.

Special care worked for me when I was in there but when I left, the world was just a different place. It was really difficult trying to settle back into everything. I didn't know what to do with myself. I ended up going wild then. I got back in contact with my old mates and all.

When I was in special care I was forced to go to counselling, and I wasn't allowed leave till I had that counselling done. I knew I wasn't ready for counselling at that time – I wasn't ready to speak about anything. And then when I left special care, any time I did speak, I went off the walls, I went wild. It was the manger of my residential who noticed the counselling was having a big impact on me: every time I'd come home from it I'd run off for days. She said it to my social worker and then I stopped going. And it's only recently, since I turned twenty-one, that I went back to counselling. There wasn't a hope when I was fifteen or sixteen of being able to deal with all that stuff. Now I know I'm ready to deal with it and I want to deal with it.

When I turned eighteen, everything changed. The first week after that it was like, you have to find an apartment, you have to go sort out your rent allowance, get onto the housing list. But I was still in education. I got an extra four months and that was it then, I was moved into an apartment on my own, and it scared the living daylights out of me. I moved out of the apartment after three months of living in the place. I overdosed. Then I tried to re-engage with the HSE. I was asking them, can I get an aftercare support? I need someone to help me get a doctor, and all that; I need somewhere to live. My request got denied and I had to appeal it and it still got turned down.

Then, when I was nineteen, I tried to re-engage with my aftercare again. Every time I rang I left a message and I was told someone would get back to me. They didn't. I'm twenty-one now and I've recently got in contact again with the aftercare services and the social work department. I asked them for funding for college, for counselling, for a top-up on my weekly money. Everything got rejected. They don't work with anyone after twenty-one. It's not nice when you can't even have someone to ring and say hello and go out and meet them for a cup of coffee like, just to check in and see how you are. Youse are after been minding us till we turned eighteen, looking after us, cooking our dinners, making our breakfast, making sure we washed ourselves, that we got up out of bed, everything – like, practically bubble-wrapped us till we turned eighteen – and then you send us out into the world on our own. The bubble-wrap is off and we're left standing there: how do I pay bills? Which money is for which? Can I afford everything this week? You throw us out when we're eighteen but you wouldn't do it to your own sons and daughters: why the hell are you doing that to us?

Mark

My ma had three kids and herself in a tiny little apartment in Ballymun. It got hard for her and she became an alcoholic. Bills weren't paid so she decided to leave and we just ended up living on the streets in Dublin city. We spent a couple of nights underneath buildings or in shop doorways, anywhere there was shelter for a night's sleep. Then we were taken into care. We were put in a residential centre in Dun Laoghaire. I was with my younger brother; I was six, he was three. My older brother got separated: he went into secure care. It was a very big house with a lot of staff; it was a terrifying experience, trying to figure out 'Why are we here?' and 'Where's our ma gone?'

We were there for six months and then my ma got back to normal and she was given a house in Blanchardstown and we went home. Everything was going well but then she just got back on the drink. There was no support there for her: I'd never once seen a social worker coming out, having a meeting, seeing how my ma was doing. One time, I was left with the next-door neighbours. My ma didn't come home for three days. And then the neighbour rang the guards and the guards took us into emergency care. My mother went missing for nearly three years after that. The social workers told us she was sick.

They couldn't get us our place back in the residential centre so we lived in Temple Street hospital for two months, me and my little brother. We were kind of freaked out for the first week we were there – we thought we were sick. Everyone in the hospital was real nice to us and after a while we got used to it. But at the back of your head, when you're in a hospital you think you are sick. Then we got our place back in the centre in Dun Laoghaire. [*Policy has changed since then: today, young children are automatically placed with a foster family rather than in a residential centre.*]

When we used come home from school we'd all do our homework at the table but you'd always have twelve kids on top of you. It was very structured: you come in, you have to do your homework straight away, then you have to have dinner. There's no leeway. God forbid if you have your dinner while you're wearing your uniform. There'd be 'settling time' or isolation if you acted up. I think isolation is gone now. Like, if you were caught mess-fighting you'd be isolated for a day and you'd have to stay in this room by yourself and you'd do work with the staff explaining why you did this and how come you felt like this at this time. After any argument that happened in the house, they would resort to isolation. You'd have two hours of 'one to one' to try to figure out what you'd do next time instead of arguing. And that would be more frustrating. You'd get two hours' cleaning work for being caught mess-fighting – sure me and my brother got that nearly every week.

There'd be staff meetings in the house. The whole staff team would come and upend your living area – your home. There'd be like sixteen staff at the meeting. And when it was over, they'd be walking around, doing things, and you'd be like, 'This is our house!' I understand that it's a workplace but at the same time they need to respect that it's our home. They shouldn't be having meetings right in front of us.

After a few years, we moved to another centre. They had 'red flag, green flag': bad touch, good touch. When we were first introduced into the house, we were sat down and they were like, 'a green flag touch is when someone allows you to give them a hug and a red flag touch is a no go'. Some of the lads used to ask for hugs. And they'd be like, 'You have to do an appropriate hug,' and the staff would demonstrate an appropriate hug and an inappropriate hug. It's a very structured routine in those houses; it's far too much.

When I was sixteen, I was connected up with a private aftercare service and they told me what would be expected of me when I moved in with them after I turned eighteen. I was still in fifth year when I turned eighteen. That August, I moved out of the residential centre and into an apartment on my own, with support from the aftercare service. Everything was going great. I was in sixth year, doing the Leaving Cert Applied. But as soon as I finished that I wanted to take a year out. I really wanted a break to clear me own head. I started a course but I dropped out after four weeks. And because I wasn't on the course any more I was discharged from the aftercare service: goodbye, you're on your own. Sign on to the dole, sign on to the rent allowance, and good luck trying to get it.

The one that caught me there was that you had to be in education to get the supports. If I had decided to stay in education, I would have got the supports till I finished. Because I took a year out all them supports collapsed and I was discharged. Some of my friends, who live at home with their mums and dads, still haven't decided what they want to do for the rest of their lives. But when you're in care, you have to decide before you're discharged. And if you make a mistake, you can't go back.

I moved into a place and was there for two months but my rent allowance didn't come through and I had to leave. I was homeless for a month or two. I went down to Dun Laoghaire County Council and told them my story, that I hadn't a family to support me. They were like, 'We've no money; we can refer you into the out-of-hours in town.' No way, I thought. I know other people from the care system have gone into the out-of-hours service. The stories that come out of it – of people's faces getting sliced open; people getting boxed around; people coming in pissed off their mind causing fights. Horrible shit, like. I stayed in my friends' houses. I found a place to live eventually.

I'm doing social studies in college, training to be a social worker. They teach you not to get attached to the young people you're working with. But when I was a child in residential, I needed some sort of attachment because if I don't have that attachment I'm not going to trust anyone. And trust is a huge thing for young people in residentials. I'm not going to talk to someone that I don't know. So the social worker has to build up attachment to make me feel comfortable. But then when I do make that attachment to a social worker, she leaves, and then I have to start all over again with another social worker, trying to build up a relationship to be able to talk to her, to be able to trust her. After the third or fourth social worker, the trust is gone: you just go, Fuck this, I don't care any more. I had between nine and twelve different social workers. Personally, I'd find it very hard to trust anyone. It's a fear of letting someone come in close – someone comes in and says, 'Oh, we'll help you out, we'll do this, we'll do that' – but you know a couple of years later they're just going to be gone back to their own families, or off to do their own thing, and then you'll be left by yourselves. And when you leave residential care all the attachments that you made in the residential centre are broken. As soon as you're eighteen, it's like, wash your hands, goodbye. There's nothing there any more. There's no more attachments.

I've been to all sorts of therapy. Play therapy, group therapy, one-to-one therapy. In all of them I was just forced to go. Every Friday I was picked up from school and put into the situation. I didn't want to be there, so I didn't really say what was on my mind. And then you've to try and explain to friends why you're getting out of class. I do understand why residential units enforce therapy, because automatically they think you've horrific problems and this has happened or that has happened. But sometimes the problems haven't been that bad. Some of the problems are solely to do with the residential unit or the social worker. Twenty different people around you that you haven't got a feckin' notion who they are. But we did know who our mother and father were; we did know who our aunties were – but they were taken from us. The therapists are trained; they've studied this: 'He's very closed off,' they say. Yeh, but I'm closed off because I don't know anyone, and I don't want to know anyone here.

In September, I joined Sarah and the woman with whom she lives, Sharon, in the district court. The night before, Sarah had lain awake till four-thirty, petting her dog and watching TV to try to relax. Eventually she fell asleep, and then slept through the alarm on her phone. Sharon woke her, and she took her time getting dressed. 'You have to look ladylike for court,' Sarah told me, later. 'You don't want to look like a skanger.' She chose a black Karen Millen top that Sharon had given her and a black and white striped blazer from Penney's, and then spent twenty minutes doing her hair. She had coffee, but no breakfast. She felt sick with nerves.

Sarah and Sharon drove together to the courthouse, where I met them. They sat at the back, watching the judge go through the list: an eighteen-year-old was jailed for six months for carrying a concealed weapon; a grandmother was fined for stealing from a shop; a twenty-something mother was told to give €500 to charity for being caught with cocaine at a music festival. Sarah's case came up, and she and Sharon approached the front of the courtroom. 'Sarah, how are you?' said the judge, with a tone of brisk welcome. 'You're still alive,' he congratulated her, with only light irony. They knew each other from Sarah's previous court appearances. 'He gets it,' Sarah told me, later. 'He gets how vulnerable we are.'

Sarah was in court on a two-year-old larceny charge. This hearing was to allow the court to review the latest probation report. The judge had provided money from the court poor box to pay for a course of counselling; Sarah had responded well, and her probation officer recommended that she continue to engage in therapy and related activities.

The hearing gave Sarah's solicitor an opportunity to raise the issue of the role of the HSE. The HSE had previously been funding a package of outreach support for Sarah, but this had been withdrawn just before her twentieth birthday. 'The State just wants to wash its hands of Sarah,' he said, 'but at the moment she's not equipped to deal with the outside world.' The judge appeared to agree. He addressed Sarah.

'I think it's tragic that you have been in care since you were in nappies and now you find yourself, at twenty, in such difficulties,' he said. 'The state effectively took care of you, in lieu of your parents, and, now that you are twenty, has decided, to use the words of your solicitor, to wash its hands of you. ... Every day I put children into care in this court. If that's what's coming down the road for them when they hit eighteen – that the state ... washes its hands – it's a sad day.'

Glacier Bay

NEIL BURKEY

I first visited Alaska during the summer of 1999, when my sister worked there. Glacier Bay National Park is a remote location, though nowhere near the remotest that state has to offer. If Alaska is Bill Clinton in profile, staring down Russia, then Glacier Bay is where he might tighten his necktie, just west of British Columbia along the stunning littoral of fjords and islands that the United States conned from the Canadians.

One couldn't feasibly not like Glacier Bay. It was a paradise of sorts. Entire flocks of bald eagles sat on the shore teaching their fat, dark young to buzz the heads of pier-walkers. Porcupines contemplated you from the branches above, slowly chewing. Moose prowled the mossy, pine-scented paths, mothers ready to charge if you came between them and their young. Fireweed rose like hot pink pokers everywhere you looked, the myth being that the coming winter's snow would pile to the same height. Here and there were dotted the cultural droppings of the natives, the Tlingit (pronounced 'clink it'), exemplars of the clean, sharp, quietly surreal artworks of the Northwest tribes, all ravens and bears and grinning wolves.

The following May, having signed up to work the summer season at Glacier Bay Lodge, I flew to Anchorage, where I was to obtain the Class C driver's licence that would allow me to operate large passenger vehicles. My sister had advised me that landing a position on the transportation team was key to a cushy and prosperous Glacier Bay summer and so that was the box I had ticked on the application form. Anchorage was an odd place: flat, gridded, masculine. Children stood on street corners turning their fists in their eye sockets, as if stunned by the dim spring sun. The Class C licence test consisted of twenty questions administered by computer, and as I had studied so

I passed. Then it was on to the capital, Juneau, a town of 30,000 that still showed its gold rush roots. It was feral and cramped and boozy, and it carried the indelible odour of fish. From there I caught a ride on a two-seater airplane, the pilot of which said not a single word during the entire trip, and so I just gaped at the mountains we were flying between and the glaciers we were flying over.

We landed in Gustavus, a handsome little town that acted as the service point to the national park. I then travelled on to the lodge via one of the buses I myself would soon be driving at my peril and everyone else's. The lodge was a 1970s bit of rustic, low in the entry but with a stilted backside beyond which a gentle slope ran some twenty yards before slipping beneath the bay. Sitting on the wide wooden balconies in the evenings, as I'd done when visiting my sister the previous summer, one could watch humpback whales make 'bait balls', swimming circles around a school of fish while blowing a net of bubbles, then gobbling them up by the thousands in a thrashing display. But the view from the lodge was not for employees. I was shown to where the staff were housed, four to a room in doddering wooden buildings hidden from tourist eyes and from whale eyes but within the moose's range.

My fellow staff members belied any lazy assumption that those seeking employment in the wilderness were likely to be of an adventurous or wholesome disposition. Most at the lodge were there only, it seemed, to make money to buy alcohol (which, given Glacier Bay's remoteness, was outrageously expensive). They would spend their summers in Alaska, drinking around campfires, singing around campfires, jumping naked over campfires, and their winters in Banff or Aspen, where they no doubt occupied themselves in a similar fashion.

A job is a job, however, and no journey in life is free, and so I drove. I drove decommissioned school buses and twenty-seat people-carriers in a temperate rainforest with intermittently functioning wipers down an unrelentingly straight and narrow road with worryingly soft shoulders, so that in encountering another decommissioned school bus or twenty-seat people carrier coming from the opposite direction you risked sliding off into moose territory.

As there was usually nothing for the passengers to look at during the drive barring spruce trees, one was meant to give a tour to (what turned out to be mostly) pensioners over a tannoy in the hopes of charming tips from them: 'Freed from the enormous weight of the Ice Age-era glaciers, the land is actually to this day still rising from the sea, in a process known as isostatic rebound – so please people, be conscious of low-flying planes during your stay at Glacier Bay Lodge ...' The only problem was that to truly cash in on the position you needed to be (or at least needed to pretend to be) the sort of person who could bear repeating the same jokes day after day, several times each day, a state I was never quite able to attain. But on occasion a moose would come out from the forest and stand in front of the bus, as if scripted by Elizabeth Bishop, and the pensioners would be pleased.

At some point in late June of that summer I had decided, for reasons I no longer recall, to give myself a mohawk – perhaps it was the glacial air. More likely it was an attempt to rile my father, who was about to pay a visit over the Fourth of July weekend. Alas, when the time came, he was unperturbed. And what exactly the passengers thought of travelling in a semi-decrepit bus driven by a mohawked young man went unrecorded, although I can say that no one refused the ride.

On the Fourth, Gustavus held a parade featuring golf carts festooned with streamers and floats with themes inscrutable to outsiders such as myself. One of the main events was a contest involving a Sitka spruce that had been stripped of bark and limbs and painted with vegetable shortening, then anchored to a bridge and dangled over a glacial river with a rolled-up hundred-dollar bill nestled into its nether end. Bolstering myself beforehand with several breakfast shots of tequila for this, the greased-pole competition, I gave it a go myself, dressed only in my mohawk and a rough cotton jumpsuit zipped tight from the belly to the neck.

For me, the main reason to be there, in Alaska, in the wilderness – the only reason, really – was for the camping. Employees were given free rental of kayaks and 'bear canisters' (big plastic screw-top containers that kept your food dry and locked away enticing odours from all but the most discerning of ursine noses), as well as free drop-offs from the tourist boats into remote bays, all of which would otherwise have cost hundreds of dollars. Often, a grizzly would be waiting for you at the dropoff point, a fact that the boat captains would usually laugh off before depositing you overboard. As you stood on the shore with the bear sniffing the air it was generally thought to be polite to wave at the boat as it steamed off to the next bay. 'Same time every day,' the captain would shout, 'and if you're not here you're out of luck!'

It's difficult, at this remove, to recall the quiet that descended once the noise of the engine had dissipated and the bear had lost interest and wandered back into the trees. My companion on these trips was the incomparable Colin Hedges from Wenatchee, Washington, a man never eager to destroy such a rare silence without reason. It is difficult, too, to describe the sort of experiences one has in a wilderness of that quality without drifting into purple prose about the breathless moments after the dorsal fin of a killer whale rises noiselessly from the water, makes a beeline toward your two-man kayak, then sinks again beneath the surface. Or about wolves howling at sunset as you drift in for a spot to camp. Or about the Northern Lights mutating from beams of light into a green curtain emanating in waves from the mountains. Or about walking on a glacier and hearing it speaking in crackling tongues beneath your feet. Or about the utter peace amongst the expiring lakes.

On one of those trips, towards the end of that summer, we decided that we would camp right at the mouth of a glacial bay. This was not necessarily the most appealing of locations, given the tendency of the terrain to be steep and stony and for the winds to be refrigerated, but we were seeking extremes at that point.

So after struggling up the sides of what was essentially a gigantic boulder sticking out of the sea to gain higher ground on which to plant our tent, we kayaked into a bay choked with icebergs. On top of most of these icebergs sat a seal and a pup, for we had just passed the birthing season and entered the weaning season. As we drifted in they stared at us with glossy eyes, waited, took judgment, and slipped into the water, one by one. We'd been warned by park rangers to keep our distance from the seal pups, as many were too young to swim and could be lost to the sea, but we had ignored them. The pull of the bay, and of the blue-white wall of ice in the distance, was too strong. When one of the seal mothers returned to the surface and started to bark in what we took to be a mournful way, we changed course, keeping nearer the mountainside, which loomed nearly vertically over the water. We paddled on, the glacier drawing incrementally closer, glowing a dirty blue. Ahead of us, a waterfall cut a slender channel down the side of the mountain. We stopped paddling for a moment and let ourselves drift forward. The mother seal by this point had ceased her barking and all again was silent.

It was then that there came a small noise from above. I looked up to see a stone approximately the size of Colin's head skipping once off the rock face before coming straight at us in a spinning blur, leaving me no time to squeak out a warning let alone attempt to paddle ourselves clear. It hit the kayak directly between the two of us with the force of – with the force of a stone approximately the size of Colin's head falling from a sheer cliff – before disappearing into the water. Colin turned back to see what the hell had happened (as well as what the hell might be about to happen) and as our kayak rocked back and forth neither of us spoke. When we did, it was to confirm that we had nearly died, but that we had not died. We agreed that, had the stone hit him, or had the stone hit me, it would have left his head, or my head, a bloody, messy pulp, and that whosever head it had not pulped would have been left between the cold wind and the seals, adrift with a corpse.

The next day, as we paddled back to the pickup point, I couldn't help but picture myself struggling across those many miles with Colin's headless body hunched over into the water as if he were looking for something there in the deep, looking for little wet seals with big wet eyes.

Notes on contributors

RACHEL ANDREWS is a freelance journalist based in Cork. Her piece on wild-fire in Ireland appeared in *Dublin Review 46*.

NEIL BURKEY is working on a novel and a collection of short stories. His story 'A Matter of Minutes' appeared in *Dublin Review 41*.

BRIAN DILLON's books include *Tormented Hope: Nine Hypochondriac Lives*.

GWEN GOODKIN is a working on a collection of short stories.

CORMAC JAMES's new novel, *The Surfacing*, is to be published next autumn.

COLIN MURPHY is the author of *Guaranteed!*, a play about the Irish bank guarantee. His piece about the history of Smithfield and its horse fair appeared in *Dublin Review 47*.

PHILIP Ó CEALLAIGH's most recent collection of stories is *The Pleasant Light of Day*. His piece about Isaac Babel appeared in *Dublin Review 50*.

subscribe to *the* Dublin Review

Four times a year, *The Dublin Review* publishes first-rate writing from Ireland and elsewhere – essays, memoir, criticism, travel, reportage and fiction – by world-class writers.

A year's subscription to *The Dublin Review* brings four issues to your mailbox for the same low price you'd pay in a bookshop. It also makes a wonderful gift – or four gifts!

Annual subscription rates:
Ireland: €34
Rest of world: €45 / UK£36 / US$60
Institutions add €15 / UK£13 / US$20

It is easy to subscribe to *The Dublin Review* via our website: www.thedublinreview.com.

If you don't wish to subscribe via www.thedublinreview.com, please send a cheque to The Dublin Review, P.O. Box 7948, Dublin 1, Ireland, making sure to supply your full address.

the Dublin Review Reader

Since the appearance of its first issue in December 2000, *The Dublin Review* has published work by world-class writers four times a year. Our anthology, *The Dublin Review Reader*, gathers a selection of the best non-fiction from the magazine's first seven years. With pieces by

John Banville   Angela Bourke   Ciaran Carson

Amit Chaudhuri   Catriona Crowe   Brian Dillon

Anne Enright   Roy Foster   Vona Groarke

Selina Guinness   Seamus Heaney   Michael Hofmann

Ann Marie Hourihane   Kathleen Jamie

Molly McCloskey   Patrick McGrath   Derek Mahon

Christina Hunt Mahony   Lia Mills   Andrew O'Hagan

Glenn Patterson   Tim Robinson   Ian Sansom

George Szirtes   Colm Tóibín   Maurice Walsh

Go to www.thedublinreview.com to order *The Dublin Review Reader*; or send a cheque to The Dublin Review, P.O. Box 7948, Dublin 1, Ireland, making sure to supply your full address.